The Solitary Twist

a Nell Fury mystery

The Solitary Twist

a Nell Fury mystery

by
Elizabeth Pincus

Spinsters Ink
Minneapolis

First edition.
10-9-8-7-6-5-4-3-2-1

Spinsters Ink
P.O. Box 300170
Minneapolis, MN 55403

This is a work of fiction. Any similarity to persons living or dead is
a coincidence.

Cover art by Miranda Lichtenstein
Production by: Melanie Cockrell   Kelly Kager
                     LouAnn Matossian   Liz Tufte

"Am I the Only One" words and music by Maria McKee,
(c) copyright 1989 by Little Diva Music.
Rights administered by Geffen Again Music & Music Corporation
of America, Inc., New York, NY 10019.
Used by permission. All rights reserved.

Printed in the U.S.A. on acid-free paper.
Library of Congress Catalog Card Number: 93-84274
ISBN: 0-933216-93-9: $9.95

For Donna

Acknowledgements

I am grateful to friends and colleagues for their ongoing support. The following people, in particular, have been generous with enthusiasm and conviviality: Tinka Pincus, the Avoys and the McKnights, Elizabeth Coffey, Teresa Eyring, Sara Felder, Linda Gutterman, Paoli Lacy, Kelly Love, Tede Matthews, Leslie Moulton, Vanessa Nemeth, Stephanie Poggi, Mary Wings, and the Sisters (in Crime).

Special thanks to Sherry Thomas, Spinsters' outgoing editor, for her spirited dedication to Nell Fury and four-wheeled transportation;

to Kelly Kager and the new Spinsters staff for their hard work and updates on the Minneapple;

and to Jennie McKnight for perseverance, a weekend in Vegas, and a song called "Tumbleweed."

The Solitary Twist

a Nell Fury mystery

1

I was cracking the spine of a new edition of *Sinister Wisdom* when I caught a heady waft of perfume hovering somewhere to the left of me. I looked up. A comely number in a powder-blue Jackie O. outfit was shoving a worn leather valise into the overhead compartment. She must have heard me sniff, because she glanced over, adjusted her smartly-cut suit, and offered just a hint of a smile.

"Ambush," she said, sliding into the seat beside me.

"I beg your pardon?"

"The scent. Ambush." Her smile widened, revealing two rows of neat teeth with a fetching gap in dead center. Her eyes were an interesting gray that looked almost lavender, and her hair was gray, too. Whitish, as if she'd been blonde not too long ago. I couldn't think of anything to say.

"I wore it when I was a kid," she went on, snapping her seat buckle shut with a metallic click. "It was all the rage on the softball team. I don't know who we were trying to impress...."

Gray Eyes trailed off, her hands flopping in her lap like a couple of trout stranded on a dock. She turned her head and fixed her gaze across the aisle. A pre-teen in a Garth Brooks T-shirt was busy shooting spitballs at a harried flight attendant. Next to the kid, a sallow-faced man sat bolt upright and scowled into his copy of *Business Week*. Gray Eyes kept staring.

I leaned forward. I couldn't see what was so fascinating. Oh well. I reached up to click on the reading light, then snuck another look to my left.

My seatmate was smiling at me again, a delicate pink flush glowing in her cheeks.

"So," I said. I started blushing, too. She really was a knock-out. "You played softball? You don't strike me as the tomboy type."

"Hmm." Her face looked almost sad. "Oh no, I'm not. But I loved playing softball with the girls. I loved everything about those years. The hot summer nights—"

She stopped abruptly, this time focusing her attention on the air-sickness bag poking jauntily out of the seat-back pocket in front of her. I was getting sick of this on-again, off-again conversation, but the Ambush was working on my synapses like a potent aphrodisiac. I figured we'd get along fine if we didn't talk. I opened my magazine and tried to read, but all I could think about was the scene in *Rich and Famous* when Jacqueline Bisset follows a stranger into the airplane toilet for a little mid-air tryst. It'd long been one of my favorite fantasies.

Gray Eyes was nodding off in her seat, a slight wheeze escaping with each steady breath. I glanced out the yellowed window and watched the boxy terminal buildings fade from sight. The plane started to pick up speed, rattling and rocking as we plummeted down the runway.

Just before takeoff, I had a vision of all the people in all the steel tubes criss-crossing the sky in random fashion, a whole network of true believers who really thought they'd get home safely to Wichita or Tucson or Anchorage or Buffalo. Or, in my case, to San Francisco, that silvery little jewel of a city where inhibitions are lowered, dreams are fostered, ambitions nurtured and—in too many cases—all hopes are dashed.

I must have dozed off, too. I felt someone shaking my arm, and looked up to see a beaming sky-waitress with a Dorothy Hamill wedge and a nametag that read "Madonna." I let her put a lunch tray in front of me. The whole cabin smelled the way my kitchenette does when I steam the vegetables too long.

Gray Eyes was asking if I wanted a drink.

I tossed a few stray curls out of my eyes. "Um, Bloody Mary."

Madonna set us both up with tiny vodka bottles, tomato juice in plastic cups, and packets of cocktail mix. My seatmate seemed to be paying attention again. She paid for the drinks, asked if I'd had a good rest, told me her name was Christa Lovett. Then I noticed she was holding my copy of *Sinister Wisdom* in the hand that wasn't cradling her Bloody Mary. The cover art was an ink drawing of a woman's genitalia against an orangy-red background—it looked like a rotting peach pit. Christa seemed entranced nonetheless.

"I haven't seen this journal in so long," she murmured, riffling through the pages that contained lesbian essays, fiction and poetry. "I hope you don't mind. You dropped it on the floor. I've been reading bits and pieces of it."

I sipped my drink. Spicy. I said: "Of course not. No problem."

The plane hit some turbulence and a dollop of Bloody Mary spilled down the front of my white button-down. I grimaced. Christa leaned over and managed to smear it around with her paper napkin until it resembled a map of Florida. I thanked her for her help. Up close, her eyes were the color of summer fog, and her perfume still worked its delicate magic.

I squirmed and told her my name was Nell Fury.

"You know, Nell, maybe you can help me." Christa gave *Sinister Wisdom* a knowing glance. "Do you live in San Francisco?"

I nodded.

She went on. "This might sound strange, but...I need to hire a private eye."

I kept my poker face while taking a bite of quiche surprise. "I've heard stranger."

"I mean," Christa said, "people don't *really* hire private eyes anymore. But I—"

"Sure they do." The quiche didn't taste like much, but the accompanying biscuit had a nice trace of buttermilk. I grinned at Christa. "Now, if you wanted to hire a hitman, *then* I'd be a little taken aback."

Christa laughed politely, took a big slug of her drink. She suddenly seemed dejected. "I guess it's foolish to ask. I just thought...I don't know." She lowered her voice. "I thought it'd be great to hire a lesbian. I thought you might

4

know someone. But that's so unlikely, even in San Francisco. I guess I'll just check the Yellow Pages."

I ate some more biscuit and ripped the cellophane off a miniature square of brownie. I contemplated the situation at hand. I'd just spent four days in Minneapolis wrapping up a harrowing case that involved a mother and child on the lam from a monstrous husband. Before that, I'd wasted some weeks on a surveillance job, trailing around a slippery bank president suspected of moonlighting on company time. That one had amounted to nothing, but I'd been paid well anyway. At the moment, all I wanted to do was take a break from the stresses of private detecting. I planned to spend a week catching up on the pennant races, reading *Backlash*, and hanging out with my daughter Pinky. She'd been living with me all summer, and was due to fly back to London in about a week to get ready for school.

But here was a flesh-and-blood client clamoring for private heat. And she wanted a lesbian, at that.

I made the brownie disappear and turned to Christa. "I'm a private investigator."

She blanched. Then she rotated slowly to drink me in, from my scruffy oxfords to my black jeans to my moppish hairdo in need of a cut. I know I don't appear very professional, or even very remarkable, but that's one of the perks of the trade. I can be comfortable, adapt to any situation, and know in my heart that I'm more dangerous than I look.

Christa started to say something, but Madonna interrupted to clear our trays. I folded up the flimsy table and rummaged through my carry-on bag in search of a business card. I only had a few left of this batch, pale pink bond with gold lettering that read: "Nell Fury, Private Investigator—'I Like to Watch.'" It was time for a fresh design. I was currently in the market for new office space, anyway, which would require a new phone, new cards, the whole shebang.

I found one and handed it to Christa Lovett. "Are you any relation to Lyle?" I asked.

"Huh? What?" She was turning the card over and over, inspecting it in minute detail.

"Lyle Lovett. You know, big hair, the Nashville sound?"

"No," she stammered. "I never...No...."

Geez. Now that she'd found herself a private detective, she didn't seem to know what to do with me. Maybe it'd just been a conversational gambit or something, a way to talk about dykes or the latest exploits of V.I. Warshawski. Or maybe she was just having another bout of spaciness.

I was about to reclaim *Sinister Wisdom* and forget the whole thing when Christa shook herself alert.

"Great," she said. "This is great. What do you charge?"

"Two hundred dollars a day, plus expenses."

I could see calculations clicking away behind her dreamboat eyes. She bit gently on her bottom lip. "Well...how many days would it take?"

I laughed and reached over to touch her hand. "Christa, I don't know what the job is. Tell me what you need done, then I'll give you an estimate."

Her cheeks pinkened one more time. "Yes...."

The story went like this. Christa's ex-lover, Ellen Norway, was now engaged to a fellow named Philip Gold. Christa didn't like him, and not just because he was marrying her former squeeze. Christa thought Gold was trouble, a two-bit hustler who was after Ellen's money. Christa wanted me to investigate Gold's background: assets, criminal record, former employment, stuff like that. Just to make sure he was who he said he was. And here was the catch—she

6

didn't want Ellen Norway to know about it.

I let a few moments go by. "And what'll you do if I find out something fishy?"

Christa replied: "*Then* I'll tell Ellen about it. But otherwise, well, she wouldn't like it if I was…meddling."

I crossed my legs and a cascade of biscuit crumbs fluttered to the floor. I slapped at my knee absent-mindedly. This was a pretty common scenario, only the players were different. Fathers often sicked investigators on the fiancés of their debutante daughters—the protective patriarchs of their dear "little girls." Or sometimes ex-spouses would do it if the welfare of the kids was a factor.

But I'd never heard of a lesbian probing an ex's engagement. I suppose it wasn't that farfetched, but I wondered if there was something else eating at Christa Lovett. Plain old heartbreak, for example.

I asked: "How old is Ellen?"

"Forty-three."

"And when did you guys break up?"

Christa tugged on the hem of her suit jacket and fidgeted a little, avoiding my eyes.

"Christa?"

"Um, it was a while back, maybe ten years ago."

"Okay. But you're still friends?"

"Yes, well…" Deep sigh. "Philip Gold is kind of in the way. He doesn't like Ellen's dyke friends.…"

Christa resumed her distracted gaze, focusing on the pipsqueak across the aisle. I sighed. I was beginning to get the picture. But I was also willing to do the job. A few record checks and routine phone calls would only take a couple of days. It might not turn out Christa's way, but at least she might start viewing the circumstances more realistically.

I told my seatmate I'd take the case. She turned to me with parted lips, a quivering chin and gratitude in her eyes, and I wondered what she'd ever done to make Ellen Norway leave her for a man.

I had a spare contract in my bag, so we did the paperwork then and there. I promised to limit my investigation to three days, tops. Christa paid a two-hundred-dollar advance in cash and told me she'd be staying at the Cathedral Hill Hotel. Apparently, her good friend Ellen had forbidden her to visit, but Christa figured if she showed up on the doorstep, Ellen would at least have to talk to her. I rolled my eyeballs at that. Christa Lovett may have been a sucker, but she was a mighty determined one.

I got a few more facts out of my client: she lived in Minneapolis but grew up in a small Indiana town. She worked for the phone company. Ellen Norway was an accountant and had been in San Francisco about eight years. Yes, she had a stash of independent wealth, too. Christa wasn't sure, but she thought Philip Gold was from Brooklyn. He worked as some kind of urban planner, and he lived with Ellen in a little stucco house near the University of San Francisco.

Christa wrote down the address and reminded me I wasn't supposed to contact Ellen.

Yeah, yeah. "Okay," I said.

We were cruising somewhere above the Sierra Nevada Mountains, heading westward towards the rugged California coast and the congested little city I'd adopted as home. I felt my insides resettle as we dropped in altitude. Christa and I kept up our conversation, but we moved on to neutral things like how lovely Minneapolis is and whether Linda Hamilton's role as a buff Super Mom in *Terminator 2* is a nod or a dig at feminism. I wanted to ask if she remembered that airplane scene in *Rich and Famous*, but before I could screw up my courage we were touching down, engines screaming and brakes burning as we tore pell-mell along a seemingly endless runway at the outer edge of the San Francisco International Airport.

2

It was 4:36 p.m. west coast time when I waved goodbye to Christa at curbside. She had declined my offer of a ride and was tugging her leather valise and a hard, olive-green Samsonite over toward a hotel shuttle bus. I watched until she was sardined inside with a gaggle of bright-eyed tourists, her throwback Kennedy-era attire in sharp contrast to the array of polo shirts, khaki trousers, and souvenir caps.

I pivoted and made a beeline for the short-term parking lot.

Ten minutes later I was rolling slowly north on 101, caught in a clog of light rush-hour traffic heading for the city. It was early September, one of our warmer months; the sky was uncommonly blue and streaked with wispy clouds that looked like white crepe-paper banners. My convertible top was down, my shirt collar flapping in the soft Pacific breeze.

KSAN spat out a warbly Reba McEntire song that made my heart ache.

When I pulled the Mustang onto Ramona Avenue I spied Pinky hunched on the apartment stoop scribbling in some kind of notebook. She was wearing the black satin jacket I'd made for her a while ago that read "Pinky Fury" across the back in pink sequined letters. When I last saw her, four days ago, Pinky had hair the color of penny loafers. Now she sported a pink Day-Glo job a few strands brighter then the lettering on her jacket. It was sprouting from her head like the leafy top of a pineapple.

Sometimes I couldn't believe she was my very own kid. I had to smile.

I jumped out of the car and gave her a squeeze. "Hiya, squirt."

"Hello, mum." Pinky's grin was more sheepish than defiant. I noticed that her lipstick went with her hair and also matched the spray of psychedelic daisies on her A-line miniskirt. I realized that all around me people were going back to the Sixties, while I was still caught in some Seventies-dyke/early-Gap time warp. I laughed.

Pinky bristled. "What's so funny?"

"Nothing, honey. You're adorable." I reached out to feel a spiky clump. "You did this yourself?"

"Uh-uh," she said. "Eleven helped me."

Eleven was a new boyfriend Pinky had acquired in the last month or so. I didn't know his real name; maybe Pinky didn't either. He was one of those nonstop talkers who had more opinions at age sixteen than any sane adult whose ideals had been knocked down a notch or two. Eleven lived with his parents in the upper-middle-class neighborhood of St. Francis Wood, but he managed to spend enough time hanging around street corners to pick up a hard veneer. I guess Pinky liked him because he reminded her of the skinny, post-punk rude boys she took a shine to in London. I liked Eleven, too. He showed respect for Pinky's poetry and a healthy skepticism about almost everything else.

Pinky closed her spiral notebook and grabbed my bag. "Come on, mum. Let's go up."

I trotted after my daughter, musing on the recent transformation. Last year, when she was fourteen, she favored black turtlenecks and a marine-style buzz. She wouldn't be caught dead in makeup. Her poems—full of beat angst and youthful outrage—were evolving as well, but I couldn't possibly categorize them. All I knew was that her poetry made my eyes tear up. And the only other writing that affected me that way was the front page of the daily newspaper.

As I watched Pinky prance up the stairs, I knew that no matter what, I'd always recognize her coltish gait and that certain way she tilted her head when she was listening intently. For the millionth time, I hoped she'd move back to the States when it was time to go to college—or to pursue the renegade life of a woman of letters.

The evening turned out to be a pretty nice affair, all around. My sometime love, Tammie Rae Tinkers, had been staying with Pinky while I was out of town. The two of them fashioned a welcome-home dinner out of spinach tortellini and mushroom sauce from Lucca, my favorite Italian deli over on Valencia Street. In my absence, they had apparently overhauled my tiny attic apartment. It was so neat and clean I couldn't find anything. Rae suggested I look in the kitchen cabinet to find glasses for the wine. Aha. I bet they'd stashed T-shirts in my drawers and the toothpaste in the medicine chest, too.

I told Rae and Pinky a little about my new case, though I'd learned to be circumspect in my handful of years as a private eye. Rae was a little sick of the whole business; frustrated at my odd hours and cagy ways. Pinky, on the other hand, could never get enough of the private eye life and was always trying to horn in on my work.

I took a swallow of Lucca red and said to Pinky, "I don't know, honey. With that new do, I don't think I can take you out on surveillance. I don't know if you can assist me anymore—"

"Mum!! Sure I can! I'll wear a hat." Pinky fumed. "Besides, this Christa Lovett thing is just a lot of boring record checks, and the like. I can do *that*. You hate that kind of thing—"

"I know, I know." I laughed. It was true. The tedious busy work of investigation was my least favorite part of the racket. I told Pinky I'd give her a small task tomorrow morning. It was Wednesday night now, and with my daughter's help, maybe I could wrap up the Lovett case before the weekend.

As we finished eating, Rae caught me up on the latest dirt in the mayoral race. Our quasi-liberal incumbent was being challenged on all sides by former allies, other party Democrats intent on grabbing the top spot. But oddly, the one pulling up hard on his heels was a former city police chief, Frank Jordan, an ineffectual bureaucrat and notorious law-and-order conservative. Rae explained that people seemed hungry for a change in leadership—and Jordan was emerging as the most appealing option. She shook her head as she said it.

Rae looked at me suddenly. She had the most arresting eyes, periwinkle-hued and perpetually wet, with a ring of thick black brush around each one. I smiled.

"Nell," she said slowly, "what did you say that guy's name was, the one you're supposed to check out?"

"You mean Gold? Philip Gold?"

"Yeah. Hmm." Rae paused and glanced back and forth between Pinky and me. A miniature furrow appeared on her forehead. "That sounds so familiar...."

She set down her wine glass and stood up. "Just a sec."

I watched her walk over to the closet and rummage through a neat stack of old newspapers. That's another thing she and Pinky must have tackled: organizing a recycling zone. Pinky started clearing plates. I waited.

Rae came back to the table clutching a copy of the *San Francisco Chronicle*. She flipped to the metro section and said, "Yeah, I knew it! I just read something about a Philip Gold. Here, take a look."

I dutifully reached for the paper and let my eyes flit to a headline about the embattled San Francisco Arts Commission. The organization was in the news these days because a city-sponsored multicultural art and theater festival had failed to produce at the box office. The Commission was accused of mismanaging funds—lining the pockets of arts administrators while neglecting to pay for publicity and community outreach. Now the city art coffers were in the red, and lots of small groups who participated in the festival were being denied payment.

Another instance where "multicultural" sounded good for PR but did nothing for those actually struggling on the margins.

I read through the article while Rae got up to help Pinky in the kitchenette. Philip Gold was identified as an arts commissioner. He was quoted mouthing some diplomatic double-talk about the Commission's integrity and a forthcoming internal audit. Gold also said he supported the idea of broadening the city's arts advocacy board, a notion that had been circulating for some time. A larger board would include representatives from all facets of city life, not just the mostly white, well-heeled crowd who frequented the Opera and fine art museums.

Hmm. Well, I suppose Philip Gold is a common-enough name. And even if he *was* my Gold, the story didn't bear much impact on my investigation. If anything, he sounded like a fairly regular guy—bland, civic-minded, self-important. I tossed the *Chronicle* back in the closet, causing the tidy pile to tumble and fan out across the floor. Ahhh, just like the old days.

Rae had to take off, so I walked her down the stairs and engaged her in an extended session of lip-locking and tender endearments. We made a Friday-night plan, and she drove away in her Bronco II. The air outside was cool now, a crisp, clean kind of cold with a night smell of salty breeze and redwood chips. Back upstairs, Pinky was reclining on her futon with a purloined book from my Favorite Lesbian Novels collection. *Goat Song*, by Dodici Azpadu. She asked me if it was any good. "Intense," I replied, walking over to ruffle her cotton-candy hair once more and marvel at my run of good fortune.

3

I was at my office the next day by 8:30 a.m., much earlier than usual, but I was still on a Midwestern time clock and eager to knock off the Christa Lovett case.

I drank some joe out of a take-out styrofoam cup and tried to focus on the blur of paperwork and mail cluttering my desktop. Pinky and I had stayed up late the night before. She had tried to explain the newest music craze making its way westward from England—the rave—but I'd had a hard time grasping the concept.

"...it's kind of communal, see. Everybody dances non-stop and it goes on all night—sometimes for days. And it's like..." Pinky had struggled for words. "Really *loving*."

"Aha. So it's a return to hippie days?"

"Welllll. Not exactly. I mean, the clothes look like that, with a British touch. Mad Hatter hats, and such. But it's modern, too. The mix is electronic, and the whole thing is influenced by virtual reality and time travel and cyberpunk. You know."

I must have looked blank. Pinky shook her head and leaned back with bemused exasperation. I thought, whatever happened to her love of jazz? Now *that* was virtually real, if you asked me.

"Okay," she went on, rallying to deal with her mother the dinosaur. "Raves are really great because everybody comes. All races and classes. At least that's how it is in England—they have 'em outside, and they're free. And it's all mixed up, all different genders—"

"Oh, yeah? How many different ones are there?"

Pinky rolled her eyeballs and groaned. "You know what I mean. Like, *you'd* be welcome."

"Ohhhh...."

I lost her when she started talking about the "smart drinks." It seems the rave kids frowned on alcohol—that was passé. They drank these electrolyte-enhanced health potions that kept them swaying to the psychedelic electronic love vibes for days on end. Amazing.

I finally had to say goodnight to Pinky. I was afraid I'd slip into nostalgia and start telling her about my own teenage years in Cleveland, when we'd drink illicit wine coolers in the basement and spin "Stairway to Heaven" over and over again on the portable hi-fi.

I sipped some more coffee. Mmm—the original smart drink. Then I spent an hour sorting the mail: bills to pay, prospective clients to contact, junk, even a couple of personal letters. I spied a return address from Italy and ripped into the onion paper envelope. It was a missive from Cate Jones, a new friend of sorts who was cooling her heels at a Tuscan villa. I'd saved her neck last year, and she'd responded by

18

lending me her vintage Mustang convertible and posting frequent contemplative letters. I wish she'd send a plane ticket, too, so I could hear her philosophize in person, against the backdrop of an Italian hillside, a bottle of Chianti at hand.

I filed the letter under "P" for personal and snagged a clean folder off the top of the cabinet. I wrote "Philip Gold" across the flap in block letters. Time to get to it.

I found a standard background investigation form in my desk drawer and jotted a few notes in the margins. Then I pulled out my file box of Important Phone Numbers. I listed the calls I'd need to make to check on Gold's legitimacy— Dun & Bradstreet, Motor Vehicles, the Arts Commission, and the city personnel office for starters. If I found out Gold was really from Brooklyn, I'd call a PI pal in Sheepshead Bay. Maybe he'd agree to take on the New York leg work. Right now, Pinky was out checking court records at the Hall of Justice to find out if Gold had any local criminal raps.

I placed a call to get an assets check rolling and was about to punch in the number of my DMV contact when the phone rang. I jumped.

I planted my heels firmly on the floor, then snagged the receiver and said, "Yeah?"

"Nell." It was Rae. "Have you seen the paper?"

"No." The *Chronicle* was still folded up at the edge of my desk. I slid it across the scarred wooden surface and said, "What's up?"

"Check out the front page. It's about —" I heard a commotion in the background. Rae swore. "I'm at work. Hang on a sec."

I cradled the phone against my ear and flipped open the newspaper. I didn't see it at first. The lead story concerned the free-trade agreement with Mexico; the other top corner was a big photo of a toddler feeding swans at the pond outside the Palace of Fine Arts. Watch those fingertips, kid, I thought, as I continued to scan the newsprint. I saw it below the fold just as Rae came back on the line.

"Oh my god," I intoned as Rae started to speak.

She said: "I know. Can you believe it? What are—"

I interrupted. "Sweetie, I gotta go. Thanks. I...I'll call you."

Rae uttered a terse goodbye and clicked off, clearly miffed at my abruptness. Damn, I could be such a jerk. But I couldn't think about that right now. I turned my focus back to the article.

Ellen Norway had been kidnapped. At least that was the cops' speculation. She'd been missing since Tuesday morning when she left her financial-district office for a coffee break and never returned. She hadn't shown up at home, either, according to her live-in fiancé Philip Gold. There was no ransom note as yet, but the article alluded to a series of threatening phone calls from a man who claimed to have abducted Norway. The news story was full of holes—no doubt the cops and Feds had squelched the bulk of the relevant details.

I got up and paced the length of the room, my eyes glued to the paint-speckled cement floor. My office was a borrowed corner of a friend's art studio, a cavernous warehouse located in a former industrial zone near China Basin. Mary painted here at night, and let me use it during the daytime. The joint smelled like acrylics, sweat, and stale smoke, but the price was right. Besides, I liked the seedy waterfront setting and the intense quiet that blanketed the neighborhood like a mantle of perpetual fog.

But Mary had found a better deal over in Emeryville. She was out of here in two months; that meant I was gone, too. I figured it was just as well. I was hunting for a real office on a well-trafficked street with a coffee shop to hang out in.

I kept pacing. Along one wall, I noted Mary's latest creation, a fifteen-foot high monolith spotted with concentric circles in hues of pale blue and gray. I stopped and squinted. Suddenly, the painting took on a new form and I saw a Cubist rendering of Christa Lovett—gray-haired and blue-suited—staring back at me from the canvas.

I gaped. Then I sprinted across the warehouse and attacked the trusty phone book. A moment later I had the Cathedral Hill Hotel on the line.

"Christa Lovett, please." I waited.

"I'm sorry, ma'am, Miss Lovett is not answering."

"Well…is she in her room?"

The desk clerk chuckled. "I certainly don't know, ma'am. She just doesn't answer."

"But she's registered there, right? She checked in last night?"

"That's right."

"What room is she in?"

"I'm sorry, ma'am, we don't give out that information."

I grappled some more with Mr. Polite, then asked him to have Lovett call me ASAP. I left both numbers, home and office.

Damn, this was too weird. Ellen Norway disappeared on Tuesday, the day before Lovett came to town. So Lovett couldn't have had anything to do with the kidnapping… could she? And if so, why had she hired me? Any way you cut it, Lovett's arrival was an awfully big coincidence.

I dialed up a number I knew by heart, the cop shop over on Ellis Street. I asked for Inspector Little. He barked a greeting into the phone.

"Hello, Inspector. It's Nell Fury."

"Fury. What's up?"

Little had held a grudging respect for me ever since I helped straighten out a bit of mob trouble in the Tenderloin last year. He didn't like me much, though. That was okay; I didn't care for him either. But I was trying a little harder these days to foster cordial relations with the boys in blue. It drove me nuts, but sometimes that pipeline of information was invaluable.

I said: "What do you know about the Norway thing?"

"*What* Norway thing? We got an international incident? In some fucking fjord?"

I knew he was playing dumb, but I responded patiently, "*Ellen* Norway."

"Oh, Norway, as in Ellen. Nope, don't know a thing."

"Perhaps you could find out—"

"Nell," he butted in, "you're talking to Homicide, re-member? All I know is, this lady got herself yanked. Miss-ing Persons is involved, the fellas at Central Station, the County, the Feds, who the hell knows who else. But so far, not Homicide."

Little was an easy mark. Basically, he gave away noth-ing for free, but he was open to a little professional barter. So even though I had no intention of squealing on Christa Lovett, I said, "Okay, listen. I wouldn't be calling if I didn't have some angle on this thing, right? So let's say you chat up your pals, find out what you can, then you and I talk again. Say this afternoon, four o'clock, at the Mission Street Hunt's?"

"Fury, damn it, what do you know?"

"About a fjord in Norway? Nothing. See you at four."
Then I hung up.

4

I placed the call to my DMV mole after all. She apparently hadn't heard much about the kidnapping, because Philip Gold's name didn't faze her. She said she'd get back to me soon with all kinds of handy info—Gold's social security number, date of birth, driving record, the make and model of his car. Oh, boy.

I still needed to know more about the gaps in the *Chronicle* story. I tried one more avenue. But Lydia Luchetti—my stalwart journalist pal—wasn't answering. Luchetti worked for a feminist monthly called *Re-View*, but she also had a foot in the door at the *Chron* since she'd started doing an occasional investigative piece for them a while back. I hoped she'd know some of the inside dirt about Norway and Gold. I left a message to that effect on her answering machine.

Then I lit out of there.

It was another warm day in San Francisco, the sun already beating a few more cracks into the Mustang's aged leather upholstery. The car had a powder-blue paint job and a black interior, and I felt almost as cool as Thelma and Louise when I bombed up and down city streets. Today I cut over to 17th and took it all the way to South Van Ness. Turning north, I maneuvered through the gnarly intersections at Mission and Market and kept going. I found a yellow zone with my name on it not far from the Cathedral Hill Hotel.

The hotel was an ugly monster that had survived a name change, a couple of fires, and a fair share of notoriety. It sat back from the street behind a circular drive, its boxy levels rising up as if guarded by a blacktop moat. I paused on the walkway to contemplate strategy before striding into the front lobby. Five desk clerks were on duty. I zeroed in on the one with the John Lennon glasses who was listlessly telling someone how to get to Sausalito.

I waited politely while she gave out directions. Finally, the tourist toodled off. I said, "Hello."

Ms. John Lennon forced a tight smile, fearing, perhaps, that I was one more yahoo needing advice on how to find the cable car turnaround or the ferry to Alcatraz.

I smiled in return and continued, "I have a problem. I was here last night on business, and I'm afraid I left my briefcase behind. In my client's room."

The desk clerk nodded.

"And now she seems to be out. I need my briefcase for a meeting this morning." I sighed theatrically and glanced at my watch. "I *really* need it. Do you think someone could let me into the room? Just for a second?"

The clerk pushed a strand of dishwater hair behind her ear and squared her shoulders. "Ma'am, I understand your problem. But we can't allow anyone into another guest's room. I'm afraid you'll have to wait —"

"But what if Miss Lovett doesn't return soon?" I blustered, feigning a growing hysteria. "I could blow this deal! Look—"

I stopped abruptly and gazed through the clerk's tarnished gold rims. Her amber eyes were flecked with spots of black. I looked down and noticed a well-thumbed paperback sequestered on a ledge beneath the counter. I read the title upside down: *Anarchy and Rage*. Clearly, Ms. Lennon's job was distracting her from more worthy endeavors.

Hmm. I wondered if I could risk it.

What the hell. Nobody was hovering nearby. I slipped two twenties from my pocket and folded them in my palm. Then I reached down and tucked them between the pages of her book.

Her eyes widened, but she didn't say anything. She stepped sideways and punched a few buttons on her keyboard. After a moment, she looked up and asked, "Lovett, you said?"

"Uh-huh. Christa Lovett."

"Room 317." She handed me a spare key and turned away quickly. *Voila. Vive l'anarchie.*

Room 317 was, naturally, on the third floor, and down a corridor towards the back of the hotel. I moved briskly. A couple of women in uniform were attending to cleaning carts midway down the hall. I passed by with a greeting and halted outside Christa's door. Nothing happened when I knocked. So I turned the key and entered.

The room was freshly made up, the cream-colored bedspread tucked in so tightly you could bounce pennies on it.

A vacuum cleaner had left tracks in the turquoise carpet. I hurriedly scanned the room, checking the closet and bathroom to make sure I was alone. Yup.

Christa Lovett was still staying here, though. At least her leather carry-on bag and olive-green suitcase were in residence, laid out neatly on a low wooden table. The closet held a few prim suits, including the Jackie O. number Lovett wore on the plane. I almost felt affection for my client when I spotted the travel-sized bottle of Ambush on the bathroom counter. It kept company with Nivea cream, a box of slender regular tampons, lipstick, a toothbrush and some new-fangled toothpaste made out of baking soda.

Well, I'd satisfied my curiosity—Lovett appeared to be in town. Perhaps she had trundled off to Ellen Norway's house, unaware that her paramour had been kidnapped. Or—?

I walked back toward the luggage, scuffing my feet through the short turquoise pile. I squelched feelings of guilt as I gingerly unclasped the leather valise and peered inside. It was pretty empty. Perhaps Lovett carried a smaller handbag; nothing like a wallet, address book, or datebook was in evidence here. Just another lipstick, a couple of stray tampons, a book of Isabel Allende short stories, a small notepad and some pens, and what looked to be an airline ticket book.

I lifted the notepad. It was blank. Then I drew out the ticket book and read the computerized flight information. Lovett was scheduled to fly back to Minneapolis on September 11. That would be next Wednesday. Oddly, she had a six-hour layover in Denver. Surely the airline could have arranged a more convenient transfer. Lovett must have some reason to stop in the Mile High City.

I was replacing the stuff when I noticed a zippered compartment deep in the bowels of the bag. I slid back the tab. The only thing inside was a passport, a hard blue book with the familiar U.S. seal embossed on the front. Hmm.

I flipped to the inside cover. There was Lovett, at least her mug from a slightly younger era, staring solemnly out from the page. The passport gave her birthdate as April 2, 1947. Her birthplace: Indianapolis. I thumbed forward to the address page. Lovett had penciled in a street number on Lyndale Avenue in Minneapolis. I knew roughly where that was. I'd gone to college in the Twin Cities and remembered the general lay of the land in South Minneapolis.

I jotted down Lovett's stats in a tiny notebook I keep tucked in a shirt pocket. Then I did a final quick flip through the passport. The visa pages were completely blank. It looked like the book had never been used. So why did she carry it with her? On a trip to San Francisco?

I turned back to the front flap. Lovett's passport was due to expire in less than three months. Apparently she hadn't traveled abroad during the last ten years. Strange, indeed, that she would carry her passport along on a simple domestic jaunt.

I was still puzzling it out when I left the hotel room a few minutes later. The cleaning staff had moved on. I thought the corridor was empty, but then I noticed a blur of movement at one end of the hall. A man in a blue serge suit was clipping along ahead of me. I sped up.

The elevator doors opened just as I began to narrow the gap between us. I sprinted, but the panels closed up again before I could slip inside. Through the sliver of the elevator doors, I caught a brief glimpse of the fellow. It was only a fraction of a second, but it was long enough to start a tingle tripping down the length of my spine.

The man had flat, expressionless eyes the color of banana peels and a boomerang-shaped scar etched high on his right cheekbone. And I could swear he'd been watching me.

I found the staircase and flew down to the lobby, but Yellow Eyes had vanished. I spent a few minutes checking the gift shop, bathrooms and exits. No luck. I went back and slipped the room key to Ms. John Lennon, who took it without comment. Then I treated my growling stomach to a roast beef on rye at Tommy's Joynt, across the street, and pondered my next move.

5

Some people think private investigation requires a lot of fancy technique. Actually, my job is about ninety-nine percent common sense. Case in point: I found Ellen Norway's office address under the "Accountants" listing in the Yellow Pages. I was on my way.

It only took me ten minutes to drive there, but I ate up another half an hour looking for a place to stash the ragtop. Finally a meter opened up. I dropped in some coins and scooted a few blocks over to Sansome Street. Norway's building was a refurbished brick edifice that sat in the shadow of an ominous rocky cliff. The Big One would surely rearrange the geography around these parts, burying the chic offices filled with designers, ad execs, and financial wheeler-dealers like Ellen Norway.

But I didn't think about earthquakes as I entered the foyer and scanned the brass wall directory. It told me Norway's firm was on the second floor. Two other CPAs worked there, too.

A couple of uniformed security guards were stationed near the company doorway when I found it upstairs. They gave me a slow-eyed appraisal but didn't stop me from entering. The reception area was as spit-shined and contemporary as the exterior of the building. Even the woman occupying the front desk looked like a fixture in this modern *thirtysomething* landscape—shiny copper hair, trim figure, an outfit in muted colors that a catalog might call charcoal, pumpernickel, and moonlight. Her name plaque read "Ms. Myles."

I introduced myself. And asked if I could speak to Ellen Norway's co-workers.

Myles gave my business card a cursory glance, then murmured something into her telephone intercom. She placed ten fingers on the desktop and rose from her chair. And kept on rising. Myles had me beat by a good eight inches. That would put her over six feet.

I smiled and tilted my neck. "Is that a problem, ma'am?"

"Well, yes, it is, as a matter of fact. The police are handling matters, Ms....Fury, you said? So any further inquiry is unnecessary."

Rats. Maybe I should have played this from another angle. But I just wanted some basic facts about the kidnapping. I didn't think we were at cross purposes here. I told that to Ms. Myles.

She twisted her long pale neck from side to side, causing her blunt cut to swirl like the hem of a ballroom gown. As she opened her mouth to respond, a figure appeared in the open doorway to the left of the reception desk and asked, "What is it, Tucker?"

The man tried to keep his impatience veiled, but he didn't fully succeed. I wondered if he was annoyed with the receptionist, with me, or with the whole trauma of Norway's abduction. I peered at him more closely. He was Black, fortyish and stocky, and looked very sharp in a chocolate-brown, double-breasted suit and a light brown silk tie with gold paisley curlicues. He treated me to a grim smile.

I said: "Hello. Are you one of Ellen Norway's partners?"

Tucker Myles blurted, "Henry, I told her we wouldn't—"

"That's right," the man said. "We have nothing to say to you, whoever you are." He looked at Myles. "Is that all?"

The receptionist twirled her hair some more and said yes. Then she asked me to leave. Henry—who I figured from the building directory must be Henry Gravatt, CPA—turned on his heels and retreated. Tucker Myles and I exchanged a few more stubborn demands. I guess she won, because I finally left.

I strolled back down Sansome wondering why Norway's officemates were so chilly to me. Perhaps they were simply exhausted from dealing with the cops and the press. Or maybe it was something else that I couldn't yet fathom.

I looked at my wrist. Elvis, the younger version, grinned up from my watch face. I kind of wished it sported the older Elvis, the one with the puffy face and the rhinestone collar. Ah, well. The King told me it was 2:55 p.m. One hour to kill.

I squandered it on a walk down by the waterfront where only half of the Embarcadero Freeway was still standing. The structure had cracked during the 1989 earthquake and was now being razed to make way for downtown foot traffic and uncluttered bayside views. For the time being, walking from pier to pier involved sidestepping demolition crews, ducking under hanging cables, and dodging concrete debris.

I made it to the end of Pier 7 and did a slow 360-degree pivot, feasting my eyes on Yerba Buena Island, the sterling spans of the Bay Bridge, the green slopes of Russian Hill and the distant rise of Mt. Tamalpais. The city was magnificent today, clear and toasty-warm, its many vistas glistening with the clean lustre of polished gemstones. Even the demolition site had a certain charm. It resembled an industrial art spectacle, an absurdist rendering of urban expansion and inevitable decay.

To hell with the gumshoe trade, I thought, fleetingly. Then I zigzagged to the car and got right back to business.

6

Hunt's Donuts is located at Twentieth and Mission, a bustling corner that features a discount clothing outlet, a barbecue joint, a burned-out flophouse, and an old-style Italian restaurant that serves a side of pasta with every main course. But the real heart of the neighborhood is Hunt's. According to the flashing neon sign of a donut dunking in and out of a cup of joe, the joint is open twenty-five hours a day. And every one of those hours, the shop is filled with loiterers who sit at stained linoleum tables tipping cigarette ash into flimsy aluminum trays.

Inspector Little was out front with his nose buried in the Style section of the afternoon *Examiner*. He looked just like a cop, his furtive eyes darting up between paragraphs to see what was happening on the street. Little's nickname was Peanut, but I couldn't bring myself to use it even though he reminded me of a shelled nut—small, weather-beaten, and uniformly beige, from his wheat-colored hair to his pasty skin to his tan sport shirt and cords.

I walked up and pointed to his newspaper. "Style, eh? You planning an image overhaul or something?"

Little creased the *Examiner* in two and jammed it under his arm. He didn't smile. That Peanut, no sense of humor. I shrugged and gestured into the donut shop, then followed him inside.

Back when I worked as a two-bit rental snoop for the Continent West Detective Agency, I learned a few things about the balance of power around town. I knew, for example, that most of the men hanging out at Hunt's were not too enamored of cops and other figures of authority. Many were Mexican—or, increasingly, from other Central American countries—and may or may not have been legal residents of this so-called "land of the free." A lot of them were day laborers who hung around Mission Street corners, hoping to find work that wouldn't get them deported for their efforts. The SFPD had suffered a slew of bad publicity recently for sicking the INS on the already struggling residents of one the city's poorer neighborhoods. For now, there was an uneasy truce in effect—or perhaps it would be better termed a standoff.

In any event, Little had told me he was a regular at Hunt's, though his aloof manner didn't seem to be doing much for community relations. People ignored him, pointedly. He ordered a black coffee and carried it to a far table. The counterwoman handed me a chocolate old-fashioned with a "Here you go, honey." I traipsed after Little.

We sat. I was midway through my second bite when the inspector said, "Okay, Nell, what've you got?"

"You first," I replied, licking a fleck of chocolate glaze from the corner of my mouth.

Little cupped his beverage in two hands and took a long, slow breath. "Fury, you fucking burn my ass." He gulped some of the coffee. "Norway's gone. We're watching her house, her office, and her fiancé's office. So far, nothing. Though a report came in that a certain punk PI paid a visit to Norway's place of employment."

I raised a brow. Yup, the forces of law and order were on top of things. I said out loud: "I wonder who that could've been?"

"Can it, Fury. What the hell were you doing there?!"

"In a minute. Continue your side."

"A dude keeps calling, says he has Norway. He's real vague and his voice is muted—and he keeps it too short to trace. Finally, just this afternoon, he started making demands. He wants the fiancé to pay out a million and a half. We're waiting on the where and when, all the details."

"Does Gold have that kind of change?"

"No way, he's a run-of-the-mill civil servant or something—"

"Where does he work?"

"City Planning, down on McAllister."

"But Norway's got money, right?"

"What do you know about it?"

I didn't answer. "If she has the bucks, would Gold be able to buy her release with a loan, say, from her bank?"

"Possibly." Little peered at me across three feet of table. "Possibly. We're looking into all kinds of ways to nip this thing. Norway's parents are flying in from New England, and *they've* got dough."

"So what's Gold doing? Like, right now?"

"He's at home waiting for the next phone call. And the daughter just got there—"

"What?"

"The daughter. Norway's daughter."

"She has a kid?!" My mouth gaped.

Little grinned. He'd one-upped me there, and he took a few moments to savor the victory. Then he wagged his head and said, "Even *you* have a kid, Miss Private Eye. It's not that unusual."

I snorted and tossed back the last tasty hunk of donut. "Okay. So...who is she?"

"The daughter? A college kid. Name of...Randy...no, no. Rosie. Rosie Norway. She was just starting her first year of school at Boulder."

"Colorado?"

"Uh-huh."

Boulder, Colorado. Outside of Denver. Jesus.

Little was swirling the dregs of his java around in his cup and watching me digest the information. I leaned back in the rickety chair and drummed my fingertips on the tabletop. Finally I said, "Inspector, you know I can't tell you who my client is. But I'll tell you this: Philip Gold may not be the aggrieved party here."

Little kept looking at me blandly.

I went on, "I wouldn't rule out the fact that Gold, himself, may have staged the kidnapping. Maybe"—I was shooting in the dark—"to bilk money out of Norway's parents. I don't know. I'm just not sure that Gold is as squeaky-clean as he appears."

Little and I batted around some more theories, and he tried to get me to spill the beans on my client. I didn't budge. But I did spin a story about Gold's function as a San Francisco Arts Commissioner, and his possible involvement in underhanded financial dealings. I was way out of line, but the more I thought about it, the more I started to wonder about Gold. Maybe Christa Lovett's suspicions weren't so farfetched after all.

The Hunt's patrons followed us with their eyes when we exited the shop a little while later. The counterwoman flashed me a farewell smile, one gold tooth glinting against her painted ruby lips. Outside, the air was a tad fresher, at least until a Muni bus chugged by and spat out a cloud of purplish exhaust.

Little and I went our separate ways, neither of us very satisfied with our grudging *tête-à-tête*. But one piece of the puzzle resonated over and over in my cluttered mind as I retraced my steps to the Mustang: Rosie Norway, Rosie Norway, Rosie Norway.

Pinky and Eleven were blasting tunes and making easy work of an onion, olive, and spinach pizza when I got home to Ramona Avenue. They asked me to join them. I said sure, but first I went to check my messages, grabbing a Bud along the way. Neither Lovett nor Luchetti had called. My DMV contact, however, had come through with the promised information. Philip Gold drove an '89 Ford Taurus, a four-door in forest green.

I wrote down the other statistics, too, and made a note to return Tad Greenblatt's call. He was the guy who first got me hired at Continent West. I'd gone solo a couple of years ago, preferring, as always, to call my own shots, but Tad still worked for the agency. He liked its air of seediness and disrepute. From time to time, he still parlayed extra work my way.

The pink-haired one and her scrawny beau were discussing the casualty count of the Gulf War when I finally sat down for a wedge of Mr. Pizza Man's best. As usual, Eleven was doing most of the talking. It was irritating, but at least Pinky seemed aware of it, too. She'd pipe up now and then with a concise comment that was more astute than a whole barrage of Eleven's ramblings. This time, they shared a point of view—they were appalled at the latest Bush administration cover-ups.

Pinky said to me: "You've heard the new reports?"

"Yeah." I tipped back my amber bottle. The Persian Gulf debacle had been "over" for almost six months, but information about the full scope of the region's decimation was still just leaking out in piecemeal snippets. According to a recent investigation, as many as 150,000 to 200,000 Iraqi civilians may have died during the onslaught. And many more survivors' lives were threatened since food and medical supplies were as scarce as ever.

Pinky was talking about a rumor she'd heard that a U.S. Census employee had been canned for writing an honest report about the war's death toll. A supervisor had allegedly rewritten the report, downsizing the figures.

I chewed some more pizza and felt a familiar slow burn eat away at the inside of my gut. Ever since those early days in January when a murderous display of muscle-flexing was described as a theatrical extravaganza, sort of a cosmically wondrous sound and light show, I'd felt miserable about this lousy new twist in world affairs. I'd hit the streets a couple of times, but I'd also felt rather impotent and inconsequential—disenfranchised. The feelings, at any rate, weren't unfamiliar.

I looked from Pinky to Eleven and back again.

"…and if he cared about human rights," Eleven was fulminating, "why didn't he intervene in goddamn Tiananmen Square? Or in El Salvador? Or in his own inner cities? I mean, Bush and Reagan were *supporting* Saddam Hussein for all those years—sidestepping Congress to provide arms…"

I had to smile. Something about the kids' anger made me feel better, almost hopeful. I swallowed some beer and got up to flip the tape. They'd been listening to old Concrete Blonde. I turned the cassette and upped the volume as "Still in Hollywood" blared out from the tinny speakers. I was dancing across the room to feed the fish when Phoebe Grahame showed up to join our ragtag party.

"Phoebes!" I went over and kissed her on the cheek, then dumped some fish chow in the bowl for Flannery and Carson.

"Hiya, Nell." She grinned at me and looked over at Pinky and Eleven. "Hey, you guys."

The evening took a different turn from then on out. The younger set was off to the movies—they may be opposed to war, but they were determined to see Arnold undergo a futuristic battle in *Total Recall*. As we said our goodbyes, Pinky whispered to me that Philip Gold was clean. He had no criminal record, at least not locally.

I could see the curiosity in her eyes as she spoke; perhaps she'd heard about the kidnapping. I told her I'd fill her in later. She and the boyfriend scrammed.

While Phoebe cooled her heels, I made one more stab at reaching Christa Lovett. Still no answer at her hotel room, so I left another message. I tried to call Rae, too, to apologize for my errant ways, but I couldn't reach her, either. Darn it. Then I rejoined Phoebe. She was coo-chi-cooing the little crimson fish, who darted around their glass bowl like a couple of jazzed-up water ballerinas. The original pair had kicked the bucket some time back, but we kept naming the replacements Flannery and Carson. It seemed appropriately macabre.

I watched Phoebe make a fool of herself, her short dark hair and peaches-and-cream complexion refracting eerily off the shiny glass of the fishbowl. People said she looked like the tomboy pilot on *Northern Exposure*, but I didn't know; I'd never seen the show. To me, my best friend and favorite ex-lover would always be a Jean Seberg knockoff with a brunette dye job.

Phoebe and I had a standing Thursday-night date. Every week, we passed the time and dished the dirt at a neighborhood watering hole. Now that Amelia's—our beloved lesbian standby—was about to close, we had to venture forth and find a new dive. Lately, we'd been getting accustomed to the grungy depths of another gin joint on Valencia Street called the Crystal Pistol. Buds for a buck-fifty, free snacks, and a pool table off a side corridor in case either of us was feeling lucky.

7

I didn't get to sleep that night until after 2 a.m. First Phoebe and I caught up on things. As a driver for the Barbary Coast Cab Company, she always had lots of misadventures and local gossip to report. But aside from her cabbie job, Phoebe told me she was waffling these days; she blamed it on her "Saturn return." I thought that sounded like a kiddie show at the planetarium, or maybe a pseudo-religious ordeal as pleasant as a trip to the dentist. But Phoebe insisted it was the key to her cosmic unsettledness. Well, that and Bush's New World Order.

I arrived home to find Pinky mooning around the apartment in a pair of plaid flannel pajamas at least three sizes too large. Eleven was gone, and she wouldn't tell me what was wrong. I asked if it was that pesky Saturn return. She didn't laugh, so I let it go. Instead, I broached the topic of the Christa Lovett case, filling Pinky in on what I knew so far about the Ellen Norway kidnapping. And I told her that the situation had become too dicey for her to be involved any longer—no more junior detective work. That made her sulk. I tried to reason with her, but she just said, "Bug off!" and tromped away to her corner of the flat.

Damn. I went over and kissed her goodnight anyway. By the time I got out of the bathroom, I could hear her breath coming out in shallow, rhythmic puffs.

My bed felt voluminous and cool when I finally slipped between the sheets. Before knocking off, I read a few more chapters of Nikki Baker's snappy debut mystery, *In the Game*. This one would definitely find a spot on my shelf of Favorite Lesbian Novels.

I woke to what sounded like strains of tortured opera pulsating through the apartment. Pinky's usually quiet voice was battling to be heard over the racket. I got up, turned down the music, and went to splash some water on my face. Padding into the kitchenette, I found coffee on the stove and my daughter on the telephone. Her hair looked especially gaudy after only six hours of sleep, or maybe it was her lime-green ribbed top, *à la* Donna Reed, that was so hard on the eyes.

Pinky handed me the receiver and headed for the front room.

"Hello?" I mumbled.

"Wake up, kiddo. I've got a case with your name on it."

"Tad." I switched ears. "Hang on."

I rummaged in the cupboard for my Emma Goldman mug. It sported two old photo reproductions, front and profile, pince-nez anchoring her solemn face as solidly as the moorings of a suspension bridge. I poured a cup of French roast and got back on the phone.

"What's up?" I asked.

"Nellie, you want some work? I've got a job tailor-made for the likes of you."

"Whoa, lucky me." I arched my back and tried to work the morning kinks out of my neck. The coffee was wet and warm going down. "Problem is, Tad-o, I'm on a case right now—and it's kind of a mess."

Not only that, I thought to myself, I'd hoped to spend lots of time with Pinky this week, and now I'd gone and pissed her off. I stared at Emma's stern visage and wished she were around to give me advice.

Tad Greenblatt was saying, "…it's an ongoing situation. Maybe it'll hold 'til next week. Think you'll be available then? Otherwise I'll have to farm it out—"

"Okay, okay." I thought for a moment, then surprised myself. "Go ahead and farm it out. But thanks anyway."

"You're sure about that?" Tad knew I rarely said no.

"Yeah."

"Okay. Want to meet for supper tonight? Just to shoot the breeze?"

"Sure, " I said, "if it's early. I've got a date later on—"

"With old Tammie Rae?"

"Yes, with *old* Tammie Rae. You have a problem with that?"

Tad snorted. I laughed, even though it got on my nerves a little. Tad thought Rae was kind of square, which was odd coming from a man who favored Frank Sinatra, three-piece suits, and martinis stirred, not shaken. He claimed he had a vintage sensibility. I thought he was mostly full of shit. And jealous, to boot. He hadn't had a main squeeze of his own for quite some time.

We agreed to meet at the Rite Spot at five. Just in case, I asked Tad if he knew anything about Ellen Norway and Philip Gold. He said no, but he'd keep his ears open. We rang off. I was heading for the shower when the phone trilled again.

I snagged it mid-ring and said, "Hello?"

"Miss Fury?"

I gulped. "Is that—"

"Yeah, it's me," Christa Lovett said. "I got your messages—"

"Where are you?"

"At the hotel. I went over to Ellen's yesterday, but I was too afraid to go up to the door. With all the cops and everything..." Christa's voice broke and I heard the muffled sounds of sobbing over the wire. I didn't think she was faking it. I sat tight.

The tears seemed to stop after a minute, but her words were shaky as she explained her worries. I murmured reassurances. And asked her what she wanted me to do, now that the case had taken on a whole different dimension.

"Well," she sniffled, "have you found anything on Gold?"

"Not yet. Except that he's got a clean criminal record in San Francisco. I'm waiting to hear back on his assets. I haven't started on his job history, personal contacts, New York pastthat stuff. You still want me to do it?"

"Oh god, I don't know. Do you think he's involved with the kidnapping? I just don't know. All I want is for Ellen to be okay " Christa Lovett started crying all over again.

"Listen, Christa, why don't we get together and discuss this? There're a few things I don't understand."

She sniffed some more.

"Like, why didn't you tell me about Ellen's daughter?"

Lovett hiccuped. "I...I didn't...I don't know. I didn't think of it."

"But she must have been a child when you guys were together."

"Sure. Of course. But Rosie's all grown up now. I...I'm not worried about *her*. Just Ellen."

"Hmm." I sighed and wrapped the phone cord around my index finger. I let it unravel. "So can we get together? Say, in about an hour?"

"Yes," Christa said. "That'd be good."

I agreed to meet her in the hotel lobby, then went ahead with my shower. Afterwards, I pulled on a clean white T-shirt, black 501s, and my soft brown ankle-high boots with the little silver buckles. I went to say goodbye to Pinky. She was making notations in her spiral notebook and eating Fruit Loops straight out of the box. She had nixed the concerto and was listening to Marianne Faithful's whisky-voiced laments.

"Honey, I'm going to take off now."

"Bye."

"Do you have plans for today?"

She shot me a withering look. And went back to her writing.

I forged ahead. "Well, I'll be back this afternoon. Maybe we can have a spot of tea."

"Mum," Pinky said, crossing her arms across her chest, "you *never* drink tea."

"I know, sweetie. But I couldn't very well invite you for shots of Wild Turkey, now, could I?" I walked over and tousled her hair.

She still didn't smile, but at least she rolled her eyeballs at me in a semi-friendly fashion.

I grinned, snared a few Fruit Loops, and was out the door.

8

My friend the anarchist was nowhere in sight when I got to the Cathedral Hill Hotel. But there was Christa Lovett, pacing the lobby with the slow, measured gait of a museum security guard. Today she wore tailored navy-blue slacks, a buttery yellow blouse, and another splash of Ambush. Her eyes were rimmed with red. I said hello and asked if she wanted to grab a bite. She nodded yes.

We settled on a newish joint up the street called the Tumbleweed Cafe. The decor was Southwestern lite—fake cowhide booths, turquoise tabletops, and red chile pepper knickknacks. It was only nine-thirty, but I got the day off to a jolt with an order of black bean quesadillas topped with sour cream and salsa. Lovett opted for eggs and coffee.

"I've been thinking," she said around bites of tortilla, "that maybe you should forget about Gold for now. And just try to find Ellen. That is, if you're still willing to work for me."

I licked my fork and rested it on the plate. "Christa, a million people are already looking for Ellen Norway. There's nothing I can do for her—"

"Is it the money? I can pay you more—"

"No. No, that's not the problem. A kidnapping involves major law enforcement muscle. They're—"

"I know that!" Lovett blurted. "But I need your help. You personally. You can report back to me. The cops..." She stopped talking.

"Yes?"

"I can't..." Again, she halted.

I sighed. "I don't understand. Maybe if you talk to them, tell them you're an old friend of Ellen's...I don't know." I looked into Lovett's eyes. "Why are you really here, Christa? I mean, in San Francisco?"

Lovett set down her coffee cup and fixed me with a steely gaze. Her lavender pupils were flat, opaque disks and her soft face suddenly tough and wary. "What?" she asked coldly. "You don't believe me?"

"Not really," I admitted. I chewed some more quesadilla and washed it down with H_2O. I kept watching her.

"Fine." She pulled out a small leather bag and groped around inside. She extracted a wallet. "I'll just pay you what I owe and we'll be done."

"Christa—"

"Just forget it!" She started counting out twenty-dollar bills.

I pushed my plate aside and slid my hand across the clean linoleum. It came to a halt on Lovett's stack of currency. The bills looked nice against the turquoise, resting there like

50

algae in a freshwater pond. I handed the money back to my client.

"Put it away, Christa. I promised you three days, I'll give you three days."

"But—"

"Really. You can pay up tomorrow night. I'll see what more I can do between now and then. But tell me this…" I paused.

"What?" she asked impatiently, jamming the twenties back into her wallet.

"Why won't you talk to the police?"

Lovett shook her head. Apparently, that was a question she refused to answer. Nor would she say much when I asked her about Norway's parents. She explained only that she'd met them, and that they weren't too fond of their daughter's lesbian past. Including any of the ex-lovers.

We were still somewhat estranged when we parted. Christa Lovett was angry at my lack of trust; I was miffed at her caginess. My *How to Become a Successful Private Eye* manual would have advised me to dump this sorry case. But my stubborn streak was winning out. So was my odd sense of loyalty to the lonely woman with the aching heart and the potent perfume that smelled of softball and summer nights.

Outside, Lovett waved goodbye.

I waved too, and began to head for my car. Suddenly, I pivoted. "Christa?" I called out, feeling just like Columbo, *sans* trenchcoat. "Just one more thing…."

She turned 180 degrees and cocked her head. "Hmm?"

"Have you been in touch with Rosie? I mean, since she's been in school at Austin?"

Christa squinted. "You mean Boulder. No, I…" Her mouth clamped shut. She brought her arm to her forehead and stared at me for a moment. But she didn't finish her sentence. I watched her turn away abruptly and weave through the throng on the street, back stiff, her gray locks bouncing rhythmically against the collar of her blouse. Hmm. I turned and walked away.

The Mustang was parked around the corner on Bush Street, mercifully free of tickets. As I bent to unlock the door, I sensed a brisk movement behind me on the sidewalk. I looked up in time to see a blue-suited man round the corner at a fast clip, his shoulders hunched tight inside his jacket. I blinked. I thought I saw a glint of yellow in his eyeballs as his profile flashed briefly into view.

I ran after him and rounded the bend. He was headed the same direction as Christa Lovett. But the sidewalk was thick with pedestrians on this block of Van Ness. Try as I might, I couldn't see where the guy had gone. I paced for a block or two, but it was no use. Old Yellow Eyes, the mystery man, was once more swallowed up by the crowd.

Or had I conjured him up all along—a fabrication, a human mirage, a figment of my fervent imagination? Something solid to fixate on in my otherwise flailing investigation?

The next several hours passed in a blur of bureaucratic inquiry. I wanted to verify a few more facts about Gold before moving on to the improbable task of finding Ellen Norway. I drove south to the Civic Center and parked near the stately old Museum of Modern Art. A horde of noisy schoolchildren in plaid jumpers clogged the intersection in front of the Opera House. Horrors, a field trip. I dodged them, crossed against the red light, and made my way down to the Arts Commission office at the foot of Van Ness.

Posing as a grad student, I gathered all kinds of printed information about the functions and responsibilities of the San Francisco Arts Commission—annual reports, budget breakdowns, mandates for multicultural inclusivity, detailed descriptions of each program area. Naturally, there was nothing included about the failure of the recent multicultural arts and theater festival, or the accusation of mismanaged funds.

A quick perusal gave me one early impression: as an arts advocacy and education group, the agency maintained a public profile of wholesomeness and upstanding civic values. It placed priorities on things like outdoor symphonies in the park and maintaining the staid old monuments that dotted the downtown stretch of Market Street.

On the other hand, the Arts Commission also helped develop live/work studio space for artists and supported community-based cultural centers throughout the city. Still, nothing in the literature suggested that the agency took anything beyond a lukewarm stand on defending freedom of expression. Relying as it did on funding from the NEA and the California Arts Council, as well as on money from corporate sponsors, you could bet the Commission exercised caution in the kind of work it championed.

No surprise there. I was just riled up over the recent decision of the NEA to withhold funding from San Francisco's lesbian and gay film festival. And even more so over the "decency" clause that all grant recipients were supposed to sign. As if decency meant the same thing to every Tom, Dick, and Mary.

Thinking indecent thoughts, I turned my attention back

to the latest annual report of the arts commission. I learned that Philip Gold was slated to become commission president during the next fiscal year. In addition, he and someone named Stan Raphaelson co-chaired a subcommittee that reviewed plans for all new construction happening on public land. The group was supposed to oversee projects and guarantee a certain standard of design excellence and artistic integrity. Whatever that meant. Current projects under review included the New Main Library, a parking garage South of Market, and a new sheriff's facility.

I asked a bubbly volunteer at the reception desk how to get more information about specific budget matters—as in how grant allocation was determined and the status of the current internal audit. She seemed flummoxed by the question. Two gaudy orange baubles hanging from her earlobes knocked audibly against her neck as she poked haplessly among the glossy materials lined up on the desk. Finally, she found the name of the staff accountant on a list inside a desk drawer. She buzzed his extension. He was out to lunch.

I pulled a generic business card from my bag of tricks— just "Nell Fury" and my office phone number—and asked her to pass it on to the accountant. She bobbed her head enthusiastically. I watched with fascination to see if bruises would appear on her exposed neck, but the earrings caused no discernable damage.

I smiled, thanked her, and headed for my next destination.

At the Department of City Planning, I unearthed some bare-boned information with a few well-placed questions. It seemed Gold was a transportation planner with two assistants, a secretary, a private office on the fifth floor, and nine years of tenure at the San Francisco agency. Before that, he'd worked for an environmental design firm in Brooklyn and received an advanced degree from Columbia University.

I gleaned these facts from one of the assistants, a loose-lipped young man with a marine buzz cut and a mouth full of shiny silver fillings. He smiled often and widely as he guided me on a mini-tour of the transportation division, blabbing freely about Gold, the intricate timing of city stop lights, Frank Jordan's commitment to free-flowing traffic, the state of the ozone layer, and the kidnapping of Ellen Norway. Phew—I thought I'd have to hear about his frat party antics, his last family reunion, and perhaps the meaning of life before we got around to the relevant info.

But all he could tell me was that Gold had met Norway three years ago at a charity fundraiser. They'd been an item ever since. He said everyone in the office was worried about Ellen and totally baffled by the incident.

Buzz Cut was remarkably uninquisitive about my own interest in the matter. So I kept playing it loose and tried to pry Gold's salary out of the motor-mouth. He didn't budge on that. But from my observations, I figured Gold was doing slightly better than Inspector Little had surmised. I figured he was hovering in the $60,000-70,000 range.

It was getting on towards three o'clock when I bid adieu to Buzz Cut. I used the pay phone in the lobby to call home. Pinky had left me a custom message saying she wouldn't be around that afternoon for Wild Turkey *or* tea—she was going to the mall with some friends. Yikes. Since when did beat poet Madeline Zule Fury—AKA Pinky—go to malls?

I puzzled over that one for a while, then pushed the revolving glass door until it spat me out onto the sun-warmed sidewalk. A flock of pigeons kept company with a well-bundled woman sitting hunched against a low cement wall. I paused for a moment, unsure what to do with myself. I sighed. Then decided to forego Ramona Avenue and make an unscheduled stop on this fair and fleeting Friday afternoon.

9

Gold and Norway lived on Beaumont Avenue, a short couple of blocks in a middle-class enclave out past the University of San Francisco. I drove there with the top down, the tape player crooning my new favorite song. I kept rewinding and playing it over and over again. Whew—that Maria McKee sure has one mean set of pipes.

Speeding down Turk Street, I blared along with Maria: "...and it *wrung* me out and *strung* me out and hung years on my face, God *help me*, am I the only one who's ever felt this way?!"

My throat was sore by the time I crested the hill near USF's Lone Mountain Campus. I rolled on in the direction of the ocean, passed Beaumont, and stopped at a corner deli for an A & W. I chugged half the soda and ran the cool can across my forehead. Then I studied my trusty AAA map.

One problem with the little blue Mustang: it's a bit conspicuous for my line of work. I decided to drive around the block and park near the corner of Anza and Beaumont. I figured I'd be able to see the Gold-Norway domicile from there. Just in case, I put the top up and donned a pair of clunky black glasses with clear frames. Soon I was going to have to get some real spectacles. I'd found myself squinting a lot lately.

I also dug around in the back for my beat-up old Cubs cap. I stuffed my mop up under the bill and felt a pang of nostalgia for the boys of summer. The season was fading fast. I hoped I could take in a game or two over the weekend and catch up on things, especially the inevitable woes of my very own Cubbies.

I found a parking place on Anza, one of those dinky slots between two driveways that forces you to leave your nose or tail hanging over the edge. I peered down Beaumont and spotted the house with no problem. It was a few doors in, a two-story stucco affair connected with the houses on either side. It had a red tile roof, brown trim, and a tidy stone garden in front in lieu of a yard. A couple of stern-looking fellows held court out front, one standing on the stoop, the other lounging in a vehicle.

I wasn't sure what I was looking for, but I knew I wanted to get the lay of the land and a glimpse of the principal players. I scanned the street. I spotted a green Taurus, parked crookedly near the base of Gold's driveway—his wheels, no doubt.

I sat. Occasionally, a car rolled down the street, either searching for parking or on its way someplace else. There was a fair amount of movement in and out of the neighboring homes. It was, after all, the end of a work week. People were returning from jobs, maybe hovering around their doors and windows to watch the action at the Norway-Gold house. I watched, too. The law enforcers held their positions. Now and then they'd pair up and have a chat. I wondered if any more calls had come in from the man with the $1.5 million dream.

Then I got a break. The door swung wide and a head popped out to summon one of the men. I squinted. It was a woman, who appeared to be quite young. Her long blonde hair was yanked up in a ponytail, a few artful bangs arching high across her forehead. She wore tortoise-shell glasses. When she stepped all the way through the door, I spied a pair of aerobicized legs poking out of baggy black shorts and an oversized pink sweatshirt. I'd lay odds it was Rosie Norway.

She retreated with one of the cops. Suddenly, another figure was framed in the doorway. He looked average in size, a little lumpy, a shock of brownish hair falling forward into his eyes. I pegged him in his late 40s. He shook hands with the other guy, then walked hurriedly down the stubby driveway. A leather case dangled from his left hand.

I listened to the steady fall of his footsteps as he aimed straight for the Taurus. Bingo. Philip Gold.

I thought fast. Either Gold was en route to a payoff—could it have come together that fast?—or he had other business to take care of. Whatever he was up to, he had the blessings of the authorities in charge. I wondered if Norway's parents were inside. Damn. I was flying by the seat of my pants one more time.

I turned over the engine and decided to worry about that later.

Gold hung a right on Anza, so it was a simple matter to fall into place behind him. I let a dinged-up old Nova slip into formation between us. But the Taurus took a quick right followed by a left, and the Nova was no longer playing our game. I had to hang tight to Gold's rear to make sure I could keep him in sight.

Traffic was moving at a clip along Golden Gate Avenue, one of the main one-way arteries that spills into downtown. I was holding tough. Gold neither sped nor lagged, just tooled along as if nobody's life was hanging on his errand. We passed a row of restored Victorians, fussy with intricate latticework and pastel paint jobs. Then a playground on the left, the concrete blob of the Opera Plaza, also on the left, and a host of state and federal office buildings rising up oppressively from both sides.

My black convertible top made the Mustang heat up like an oven. A trickle of sweat meandered down my back.

At Hyde Street, my quarry turned right and kept going, across Market Street. A white paneled van blocked my sightlines for a moment. But I did some fancy lane-switching and picked up the tail again near the corner of Folsom and 8th Street. I was starting to feel nervous. If this was a payoff, and any cops were keeping watch, they were doing a better job of being inconspicuous than I was. Gold turned left again at Harrison.

Then he rounded the corner onto Tenth and pulled up to a meter. I drove by and stopped in a loading zone. I swiveled my neck in time to see Gold—briefcase in hand—jaywalk and follow a dirt pathway along the side of a sprawling construction site. I stepped from the car and retucked a stray curl into my baseball cap.

Just up the road from me, a droning disco pulse emanated from the Eagle, one of San Francisco's premier leather bars. I glanced at the row of motorcycles lining its sidewalk. A trio of mustachioed men headed inside, the last one flashing two pale moons through the cut-outs of his chaps. I trotted the other direction. I passed an auto parts shop and a self-service car wash. Then I weaved across traffic and entered the construction site from another side, keeping a maze of girders between myself and Gold.

Ultimately, I couldn't see very much, and what I did witness seemed innocent enough. Gold spoke to a lumbering dark-skinned man in an orange hard hat and showed him some papers from the briefcase. He passed over a manila envelope. Hard Hat glanced at the contents, shoved them back inside, and tucked the envelope down the back of his pants like Dirty Harry securing a spare Smith & Wesson. Then he lit up a smoke. He and Gold walked toward a section of concrete foundation and kept up their conversation. Meanwhile, other laborers bustled around them, hauling equipment and maneuvering beams.

As I continued skirting the edge of the site, I noticed a large rectangular sign announcing the glorious development in progress: Budget Barn.

Aha. I remembered reading about this. Budget Barn was a discount enterprise similar to wildly successful suburban stores like Price Club and Costco. But plans for this urban venture had met with some opposition. For one thing, Budget Barn was a notorious union-buster. They only hired part-time workers and offered low hourly wages with no benefits.

In addition, some people south of Market feared that Budget Barn would clog the streets with traffic, create a parking nightmare and undercut the profits of many small businesses in the neighborhood. Though by no means satisfactory to all, one compromise had eased Budget Barn through the city approval process—they'd agreed to help finance a public parking garage. It would be built adjacent to the new store.

And it was the very garage plan Philip Gold was overseeing in his role as an Arts Commissioner.

I sighed. Here I was, traipsing around in disguise like a bumbling spy out of *Get Smart*, and Gold was just conducting a little city business. I headed around the perimeter, trying to pretend I was taking a shortcut to another auto supply store over on Harrison. When I got there, I lingered in the doorway for a while watching Gold and Hard Hat interact. Nothing changed. Nobody paid me any mind. Probably figured me for Agent 99.

Elvis said it was 4:55 p.m., so I hightailed it out of there. Time for my rendezvous with Mr. Tad Greenblatt.

The Rite Spot was a deceptive little hole-in-the-wall at the corner of Seventeenth and Folsom. The red vertical sign over the door was chipped and dirty. The two cement flanks of the restaurant/bar offered no clue about what went on inside. But once you stepped through the white portholed doors, you were in an art haven of sorts: a plain rectangular room with foam green walls, an array of framed paintings hanging every which way, and a clientele that smacked of bohemian *je ne sais quoi*.

For some reason, the Rite Spot never seemed pretentious. When I got there at five after five, a skinny guy in a black corduroy shirt was working the keys of the tinkly corner piano, lilting, "Fly me to the moon…"

No Tad Greenblatt. So I went back out to fetch a newspaper, then settled in to see what I'd been missing. The big news was Joe Montana's elbow. The 49ers' star quarterback was out for the season, and the front page was overrun with intricate diagrams of his tendons, ligaments, and bones. Many column inches were devoted to speculation over his medical fate. Hmmm, I thought, they neglected to give us details about his bowel activity, hangnail condition, and astrological profile. Sloppy.

I shook my head and flipped through the news section. Montana's health had, so to speak, elbowed out news of the dissolution of the USSR, the growing turmoil in Haiti, and mayoral hopeful Frank Jordan's recent surge in the polls. I shook my head some more and kept flipping. Nothing whatsoever on the Ellen Norway kidnapping.

By the time I got to the Sporting Green, I was ready for some good news. But all I found was more on Montana and a short mention of the Cubs' five-game losing streak.

I was moving on to my second beer when Tad made an appearance. He bellied up to the bar and threw one bear-like arm across my shoulder. Flashing a sheepish grin, he said, "Hiya, Nell."

"Tad-o." I smiled in spite of myself. "You're late."

"Sorry." He plopped onto a stool, careful to keep his cuff-linked wrists free of the slightly damp bartop. "Wanna move to a table?"

I laughed. We relocated and ordered supper. I gave him a sketchy rundown of the Lovett case as we waited for our meals. Tad didn't know anything further about the kidnapping. Though when I mentioned Budget Barn, he said he remembered Philip Gold's name from the papers. Apparently, Gold had been a key facilitator of the parking-garage compromise. Tad promised to see what else he could find out.

The waiter who brought our food wore a Black Power T-shirt and at least ten silver hoops in the arc of his left ear. I thanked him for my chicken-breast sandwich. Tad had ordered lasagne *and* a burger. Tad's a big guy with a pugilist's nose and a set of formidable eyeballs that scare people who don't know him so well. To me, he's a pussycat.

As we tucked into our Rite Spot cuisine, Tad Greenblatt of the mighty Continent West Detective Agency exchanged shop talk with me, a humble lone-wolf private dick. By the time we headed outside, the sky had darkened to a dusty gray. We made a date for the Giants-Cubs game on Sunday afternoon and parted at curbside.

10

I was due at Rae's at 8:30 p.m., which gave me just enough time to stop at home and freshen up. Pinky was still out. I fretted a little, then figured that malling must hold all kinds of secret attractions I just didn't know about.

I wrote Pinky a note, checked my phone messages and rifled through the day's mail. Nothing that wouldn't keep. Then I brushed my teeth, ran a comb through my mop, and traded my grimy T-shirt for a V-neck sweater the color of smoke.

As an afterthought, I dabbed a little of Pinky's Chanel #5 at the base of my neck. It wasn't Ambush, but you had to start somewhere.

Rae wasn't home when I made it to 250 Page Street. That was okay; I knew she had a dinner meeting with some colleagues. Rae had just finished a master's degree in environmental engineering and worked as a consultant for neighborhood recycling programs. She was in the market for something new, though, something more challenging. I'd heard that refrain before.

Fortunately, she and I had been together long enough to trade apartment keys. I let myself into the studio and clicked the door softly behind me. Just being at her place brought a cloak of loneliness settling heavily across my shoulders. Loneliness for *her*. Somehow, in our year and a half of romance, we had stayed so determinedly independent that we seemed to know less and less about each other as time went on.

I walked slowly across the gleaming hardwood floor, sidestepped the Murphy bed, and halted by the window. On the sill, Rae had positioned a single rose in a slender silver bud vase. Its studied starkness matched the rest of Rae's minimalist aesthetic. I sighed. Sometimes her fastidiousness irritated me; other times I found it charming.

Tonight it seemed endearing. The rose came with a brief note on fancy ecru paper that let me know she wasn't too mad at me. I sighed again. I had to do something about my dogged single-mindedness, my bouts of carelessness that so often screwed up my affairs of the heart.

But maybe that's how it ought to be. I glanced out Rae's window. The white steeple of the church next door loomed sharply in the forefront. Its pointy peak looked almost cartoonish against the luminous blue-black sky. Just beyond, the concrete mass of Highway 101 shot horizontally across the cityscape, elegant and immobile as the hull of a docked ocean liner.

I turned away and brooded. Aside from my years with Caroline Zule, Pinky's co-parent, I'd always been a solitary creature. And even with Caroline I'd felt a little restless, a little phony, like it ought to be someone else at age twenty-one living in London with a toddler and a full-time squeeze. When we finally split after five years, Caroline blamed our age difference and cultural gulf. She was a middle-aged Jewish philosophy professor from north of London. I was twenty years younger, a middle-class Cleveland kid with a vague Catholic/WASP heritage and no discernible ambition.

I knew that no matter what our backgrounds, it was time for me to move on. Above all, I wanted to be alone. We agreed to share custody of Pinky and amiably went our separate ways.

Since then, I'd been a happy clam, at least in the love department. Footloose, adventurous and—as Tad liked to allege—quick to find perverse solace in nursing minor heartaches.

I smiled and wandered into the kitchen area. Rae kept a stash of A & W root beer in the fridge, just for me. Maybe solitude wasn't that important, I thought, cracking a can and looking fondly at Rae's tidy alignment of Fiesta dinnerware in her glass-fronted cabinet.

I moseyed back to the main room, dropped the Neville Brothers into her tape deck, and hit the play button. Then I settled in to wait.

Rae got home just before nine. She looked awfully sophisticated in a long slim skirt, sleeveless white blouse buttoned to the neck, and a generous swath of persimmon lipstick. I went over to smear it around. Rae's eyes were crinkly at the corners and her touch as welcome as the first cup of morning coffee.

We smooched for a while standing up. Then she waltzed

me over to the black iron-framed bed that was permanently unfolded from the wall. That was okay with me. Rae and I often took advantage of its horizontal position.

Like right now, as I rolled her over and pressed a thigh hard against her hips. We hadn't yet said a word, but that didn't seem to matter. I ran a hand down the side of her cheek and along the underside of her arm that was twisted up above, gripping the bed frame. I kissed her again, this time pinning her free wrist with one hand and groping her waistband with the other.

She arched. A bolt of fire coursed from my throat to my groin. We rolled sideways, and now Rae was the devilish one, toying with my button fly and tracing the edge of my ear with her tongue. I made some noise. She managed to pull off my sweater and force me back onto the satiny coverlet. I stared into her liquid eyes. In the diffuse light of the bedside lamp, Rae's face looked pale and melancholy, her blunt hair as dark as eggplant.

While I watched, Rae slowly released one pearl button after another until her blouse fell fully open. She shrugged it off.

I took some breaths, then reached up to stroke her. As she leaned forward, I let my lips travel from the base of her throat to the hollow of her breasts. She tasted salty and familiar, which suddenly made me laugh and hug her really hard. Rae struggled playfully, forcing a knee between my legs. We still wore jeans and a skirt, respectively, but we hurriedly tugged them off.

We both wore bras, too. I loved that. It seemed so marvelously slutty, two chesty gals romping on a bed in lacy underthings like Liz Taylor in *Butterfield 8*. Rae was finally pulling off my Jockey for Hers, letting her fingertips dally in the inner crease of my thigh. I could hardly stand it. When she pressed her tongue against my vulva, I gasped and had a crazy hope that time would simply freeze. It didn't. Less than a minute later, Rae's fingers working magic within me and her mouth a steady pleasure without, I came in a wash of wetness and gratitude.

Rae smiled and wiped her mouth on my sweater. Then she snuck up and folded herself against me.

Whew—this nonverbal communication sure had its moments. I kissed Rae all over and ran my fingers rhythmically up and down her back. Finally, I unhooked her bra and felt the weight of her breasts fall against me. I held her for a bit longer, then reached under the bed and extracted Rae's new favorite sex toy. It was shaped like a corn cob.

Some time after that, both of us sticky and sated, we sat up in bed and shared a glass of brandy. Rae had dug out T-shirts for us to throw on. Mine read "Better Dead Than Coed," an old Mills College rallying cry. Rae's was plain navy blue with the sleeves shorn off. She looked adorable.

I told her the latest on Christa Lovett, and about my dinner with Tad. I felt slighty giddy—happy to be in Rae's good graces and momentarily free of troubling thoughts. I kissed Rae on the mouth. She kissed me back, then looked away.

"Nell." She started twirling a strand of my hair, but her eyes were elsewhere, surveying every corner of the small studio. "Nellie…"

"What?" I sipped some brandy and gripped the base of the glass.

She looked me full in the face. The sadness was there again. I looked down and studied the trio of ice cubes bobbing forlornly in the amber liquid. Uh-oh.

I set the glass on the floor. "What's up, Tammie Rae?"

"Nell." Her voice quavered. "I'm taking a job out-of-state." Then she started crying.

Terrific. I leaned back and noticed a wisp of spider web clinging to the speckled ceiling. I felt shock. Then disappointment. For a moment I even felt relieved. Then I became angry.

I said: "And you weren't going to tell me?"

"I *am* telling you."

"I mean, before you made up your mind?"

"Damn it!" Rae sat up and swiped at a tear. "You never let *me* in on anything. And it's not like we make decisions together. I told you I was looking for work!" She sprang up and clomped into the bathroom.

She was right. I told her so when she returned with dry red eyes and a freshly scrubbed face. I explained I was a bit of a jerk about these things. "Yeah," she said, "you are." Then she sighed a little and told me the whole story.

She'd been offered an engineering job by the state of Tennessee. The plans had been finalized at tonight's dinner. It was a one-year project, so she might return to the Bay Area when it was over. Or she might not. Rae would live in Nashville, not far from where she grew up. She still had relatives there, and friends, and the job was a real coup. I nodded as if it all made sense, but really, none of it did.

I found the brandy and took a swig. It tasted watery. I asked: "When do you leave?"

"In a week. I'm driving the Bronco across the country."

"A week?!"

Rae nodded.

"You're giving up your apartment?!"

"No. I found a student to sublet it."

"Phew-w-w!!" Somehow that seemed incredibly important. And not just because of rent control. Rae laughed and reclaimed the brandy.

I said, "I love you, Tinkers."

"I love you, too."

I never stayed out overnight when Pinky was in town. Still, when I got ready to leave this time I felt awkward, bereft, as if some irreparable shift had occurred. Well, I suppose it had. I felt cut loose. And I wasn't sure if I liked it.

Rae made me keep the Mills T-shirt. Then she gripped me for the longest time. It was just past midnight when I finally drove the few short blocks to Ramona Avenue, guided more by instinct than conscious design.

11

I dreamt I was kissing Cher, pre-nose job. I was whispering sweet nothings in her ear when suddenly it wasn't Cher anymore but a blonde-tressed morsel in a latex catsuit who, oddly enough, resembled Michelle Pfeiffer. Then all of a sudden it was Rae in fringed cowboy garb! Just as I was about to unfasten her string tie, the phone rang.

I opened my eyes. There was no light shining through my postage stamp window. I craned my neck. The hands on my travel alarm glowed at 3:25 a.m. Damn.

I heard Pinky croak, "The phone's ringing!!"

If I let it go, the machine would pick up the message. But who would call at this godawful hour? I stumbled into the front room and intercepted on the fifth ring. "Hang on," I said groggily, fumbling around to turn off the answering machine. "Hullo?"

"Nell!"

"Yeah, what?" If it wasn't one of my dream dates, I

didn't want to be bothered.

"Nell, it's Lydia. Are you awake?"

Oh god, Lydia Luchetti, do-good journalist about town. She was a friend, but also a royal pain in the neck. She was the most tirelessly earnest person I knew.

"No, I'm asleep. What do you want?"

Luchetti groaned. "Give me a break, Nell. You asked me to call. I have to—"

"Yeah, I did. But not at three-thirty in the—"

"Nell. Shut up. Gold's dead."

I almost dropped the receiver. I whispered, "What?"

"Philip Gold. I just got a call. I'm on my way."

"Who—"

"The *Chron*. They picked it up over the wire and they want me to cover the story. Isn't that great?"

Hmm. Somebody died and it was a career boon for Ms. Luchetti. What the hell. I was picking up a little spare change on the Lovett-Norway-Gold thing myself, and I still didn't know what was going on. I said: "That's swell, Lydia. Now take it from the top."

"I've gotta run, Nell. But here's the gist of it...."

Luchetti explained that a foreman had found Gold's body late last night at the 10th and Harrison construction site. He had been bludgeoned with a heavy object. Cause of death: either that or the broken neck he sustained when he fell. Cops were on the scene now.

Luchetti said she'd been doing an investigative piece on the Arts Commission brouhaha anyway—now her curiosity about Gold was really piqued.

"...so I'm on my way," she concluded.

"Lydia, thanks for calling. Really."

"You owe me one." She clicked off.

I dashed around looking for clothes. I pulled on the Mills shirt, a pair of rolled-up oversized blue jeans, and my trusty oxfords. I made a quick foray into the bathroom, then ran into Pinky as I was searching for a jacket.

"Honey," I said, squishing her in a hard hug.

"What's going on?" She wore the old Pebble Beach sweatshirt I'd given her, already a hand-me-down from my brother Harry, the golf pro. Her hair glowed in the dark.

"I've gotta go out. Will you be alright?"

"Mu-u-u-ther. What do you think? So where're you going?"

We shuffled back to the front room and sat down. I told her about the D.B.

"The what?" Pinky asked.

"The dead body."

I watched her eyes open wide as quarters. There was a glint in them, too, that I'd seen before—a "take me along" glint. I cut it off.

"Honey, I'm sorry, you've got to stay home. It'll just be…you know, cops." I shrugged.

Pinky didn't get sullen this time. She just nodded briskly and made me give her the scoop. I told her what I knew, which helped clear my own thoughts. Then I hugged her again.

"Did you have a good time tonight?" I asked.

"Uh-huh."

"Did you…buy anything?"

Pinky chuckled. "Nope. We just hung out."

I nodded wisely. Of course. "And Eleven?"

"What about him?" *Now* she turned sullen.

"Was he with you?"

"No friggin' way."

I let a beat go by. "What happened, Pink?"

She stood up and turned away, pulling the sleeves of her sweatshirt down over her wrists. They were stretched out so far it looked like a straitjacket. She mumbled something that I couldn't hear. Then a siren broke the night's calm. When the whir of noise had passed, I heard Pinky crying.

Damn. I wasn't the only Fury with a bad case of heartbreak.

But Pinky still wouldn't talk about it.

"Pink," I ventured. "Do you want to go out to breakfast when I get back?"

She nodded mutely.

"Spag Wag?"

She made a guttural noise. "Uh-uh."

Spaghetti Western was her favorite restaurant, but I guess she didn't want to be seen there with her ancient mom. Or maybe she wanted to avoid Eleven at all costs. He was known to frequent the Lower Haight hotspot with the urban-cowboy–punk motif.

I told her we could decide when I got home. Then I bundled up and made for the Mustang, my own little punk–cowgal–city-slicker vehicle. The D.B. was waiting.

I listened to lite-rock radio as I wended my way through the darkened streets of San Francisco. It was a habit I had picked up from Phoebe Grahame, a woman not ashamed to be a dork. Otis Redding was sitting by the dock of the bay. Mick Jagger was waiting on a friend. And Sam Cooke and I were twistin' the night away.

I shared the city with slow-cruising taxicabs, speeding

76

carloads of kids, and an occasional gaggle of nightcrawlers streaming in or out of a late night club. As I neared the corner of 10th and Harrison, I realized I was also losing sleep with a bevy of city personnel. I spotted an ambulance, a coroner's van, at least four black-and-whites, and a handful of unmarked cars. The Fourth Estate was on the scene, too. The sky was black, but the future site of Budget Barn was awash with red, blue, and yellow lights competing for attention. On another occasion, it might have looked festive.

I left the car near the leather bar and retraced my earlier steps. I passed the green Ford Taurus. It was parked around the corner from where Gold had left it earlier. Hmm.

Most of the current action was happening a football field away from where I'd seen Gold and Hard Hat that afternoon. I walked toward the light, feeling like a mosquito about to get fried by one of those patio bug zappers. When I got close, I spied Peter Little right away, but no Luchetti.

He saw me, too, and groaned audibly. "What are you doing here, Fury?"

"Looking for an all-night donut shop. How about you?"

Little's fellow public servants looked at me curiously. He stepped away from the crowd and drew me over behind a steel girder.

The next thing he said was, "Who's your client?"

I shook my head and plied him with my own question. "Any suspects?"

"Nell. Listen up." Little was wearing beige again, this time a shapeless raincoat with a green corduroy collar. "We're talking homicide here. You don't want to rat on your client? Fine. Then scram."

"Hang on," I said to Little's back. He rotated. "Is the foreman around? The one who found Gold?"

Little jerked his head towards one of the black-and-whites. The guy sat in the front seat talking to a uniform. His door was hanging open, so I got a good look at his profile. The orange hard hat was gone, but it was the same man, alright. In the flashing strobe of the cop cars, I thought he looked Latino and young, maybe mid-twenties. I called to the inspector, "What's his name?"

Little just kept walking.

I still didn't see Lydia. Or a corpse, for that matter. I wandered over to a Channel 5 eyewitness news van. I ignored the coifed bombshell in heels and eyeshadow who was positioned importantly in front of some flapping yellow police tape. Instead, I approached a cameraperson with a load of equipment hoisted shoulder-high.

The technician lowered the cumbersome rig. Yee haw, it was a woman. She wore a faded denim workshirt, a down vest and a silver labyris in her left earlobe. "Hello," I said.

She smiled. "Indeed."

I shook her free hand and turned nervously away from her gaze. Then I made a sweeping motion with my right arm and said, "So, what are you shooting here?"

If she wondered why a bleary-eyed citizen was asking questions at a murder scene before sunrise, she didn't ask. She just replied, "The station wants footage. You know, for the 6 a.m. news." She chortled cynically. "Even though there's nothing to see."

"Did you get a look at the body?"

Now she peered at me quizzically. I noticed she had a cleft in her chin and a set of finely-arched eyebrows that met in the middle. "Yeah," she answered simply. Her smile told me she was toying with me.

I smiled, too, and coughed up a business card. "I just

want to know how he died, what time, all of that. Maybe you heard some of the dirt...." I pointed to the throng of cops. "You know."

She nodded. "Nell Fury, eh?" Then she twisted her neck to the left. "Over there. He was lying face down on a concrete slab. His skull was bloody, his neck broken."

Her smile vanished. But she continued: "They took a lot of photos, then moved him to the coroner's van. The police don't seem to have a clue. The body was discovered at one in the morning, but somebody said he'd been dead for hours."

Hmm. I wondered what Hard Hat had been doing here in the middle of the night.

I asked: "Did you overhear anything about a kidnapping? Of the guy's fiancée?"

"Oh, yeah, I read about that in the paper. Yeah, that's a weird thing. One of the cops was saying that the ransom money was ready. The guy was supposed to do the hand-off on Saturday night."

Jesus. Philip Gold was going to shell out for Ellen's return, but got iced before he could do it. That made no sense—the kidnappers would have nabbed their payola first. So was it the foreman? What motive could he have to knock off a mild-mannered transportation planner?

Then again, maybe Gold was anything but mild-mannered.

A whistle pierced the air. The camerawoman and I looked up to see an officious producer-type with a clipboard and a bad haircut bustling our way.

"Princess," he barked, "set it up!"

I blinked. "You let him call you 'princess'?"

She turned up one corner of her mouth. "It's my name."

I stared as she lifted the equipment into position. The woman was maybe 5' 10", with gelled hair, dramatic cheekbones, and a set of muscles rippling beneath her blue denim. "Princess?"

"Well, it's my nickname. Really, it's Diana, but...Princess stuck."

I felt my cheeks heat up as I watched her work. I'll be darned. Then I nodded goodbye and threaded slowly among the congregated masses. The foreman was still deep in conversation. The way Little stood by proprietarily tipped me off: I wouldn't get a chance to chat with old Hard Hat tonight.

I backtracked across the treacherous ground, keeping my eyes peeled for random potholes and other hazards. I slowed when I neared the site of Gold's rendezvous with the foreman. Luckily, I'd brought along my portable Harriet the Spy all-purpose tool—combination bottle opener, corkscrew, jackknife, pen light, and screwdriver. I whipped it out of my pocket and flashed the light towards the earth.

After ten minutes of scouring every mound of dirt and debris in the vicinity, I'd found nothing of note. I scuffed my soles around the area some more, uncovering cigarette butts, rusted bits of metal, and a discarded lottery ticket. Another piece of paper fluttered out. I bent down to take a look. It was a small bit of notepaper ripped diagonally with a phone number penciled across the bottom.

I picked it up. It looked like a name had been printed above the seven digits, but the rip had torn away most of it. The first initial could be any letter with a single vertical slash: F, I, P, etc. There were a series of curly marks beside it, but they weren't formed enough to help me piece together a name.

I put the note in my pocket along with my spy tool. I'd forgotten my watch, but from the glow on the horizon I guessed it was after five. I rolled my head around on my shoulders to try and loosen up some of the stiffness. Then I aimed for the car, watching the sky lighten ever so gently behind the raised highway and flat industrial buildings that marked this time-worn section of the City That Knows How.

12

Pinky would still be sleeping, so I decided to stop at my office before returning home. I must have just missed Mary. When I entered the warehouse, the stale odor of Camel straights dominated the air like the smell of sweat and patchouli at a Dead concert. I looked around but couldn't see any new artwork.

Maybe Mary'd had a bad night. She once told me she suffered from something called "painter's block," a condition that entailed smoking endless cigarettes, blaring head-bashing grunge rock, pondering the meaninglessness of the universe, and Not Painting. I'd been known to do all those things, too, but I didn't have a fancy name for it. I just called it depression.

I didn't think I could make it until breakfast, so I'd stopped on the way for Fig Newtons and a take-out coffee. I carried the items over to my magenta leather easy chair and juggled them carefully when I sat down. The chair had seen better days, but it sure was cozy. I sipped coffee and munched a few fig bars. I closed my eyes for a moment, but it was too inviting, so I sat up again and moved to the desk. I finished every drop of convenience store brew, then stashed the remaining Fig Newtons in a drawer.

Mary had piled a few pieces of mail on my desk corner. Among the otherwise inconsequential items was a final check from the lawyer I'd assisted on that Minneapolis child abuse case. I pulled out my rudimentary ledger book and did a quick calculation. No matter what happened with the Lovett case, I was sitting pretty comfortably. I could already cover October's bills, and it was only early September. Ahhh. This was a rare state of affairs for the likes of me.

I fantasized for a moment about a new office space, maybe a quaint cottage high on Russian Hill accessed by a set of wooden stairs—something straight out of Armistead Maupin. I thought about visiting Tammie Rae Tinkers at her new digs in Nashville. And maybe a trip to London. Then I forced myself to come down to earth. A windfall like this was uncommon in the private eye biz. My luck could just as easily turn.

I shook my head and reached around to the phone machine. The Dun & Bradstreet rep had called back. He said he would put a full report in the mail, but he gave a brief rundown over the machine. Philip Gold's credit was good. And according to their research, he was comfortably solvent with a portfolio of tame investments.

In other words, nothing to suggest Gold had reason to marry for money. On the other hand, he was no jet-setting millionaire.

I listened on. Harry Fury had called. He rambled for a while, exhorting me to come down to Monterey for a visit.

Another beep. I heard some static, a bit of mumbling, then a click. Beep. Then a male voice said, "Nell Fury? Hi. I want …I mean, we need to talk. I got…shit." Click.

That was strange. I rewound too far and listened to my brother all over again. Then the static and the stranger. I re-wound again. I still didn't recognize the man's voice. Nor could I tell why he'd hung up. He sounded more aggravated than threatened.

Well, maybe he'd phone again. I pulled the scrap of pa-per from the construction site out of my jeans pocket. I didn't recognize the three-digit prefix. It was way too early to call, so I turned to my criss-cross directory. No listing in the city. I tried Marin County. Nothing. South Bay. Nope. Then I turned to the East Bay criss-cross and struck pay dirt.

My mystery phone number belonged to someone named Sue Ann Paige. So much for the vertical slash theory. The directory put her at 279 Adams Street in Oakland. Hmm. I dug through my shoe box of assorted maps until I found the right one. I spread it out over the desktop and had no trouble finding Adams Street. It was located towards the north end of Oakland in a neighborhood of winding streets adjacent to Lake Merritt. I circled it with a pencil, wondering if Sue Ann Paige had any connection to the missing Ellen Norway, the dead Philip Gold, or the big man in the orange hard hat.

I put all my stuff away and filled out a deposit envelope for the paycheck. On the way home, I fed it to an ATM ma-chine. There was no place to park on Ramona, so I left the Mustang around the corner on Dolores. I dragged myself wearily upstairs to my attic hideaway and found Pinky Fury wide awake, demonstrating yet another facet of her wildly eclectic musical tastes.

"What the hell is this?!" I yelled.

"L7!"

"What?!"

Pinky shouted: "L7! You'll like 'em, Mum. They're women."

You could've fooled me. All I heard was the crash of discordant guitars and inaudible shrieking voices. "What're they singing?" I asked.

"I'm packin' a rod! I'm packin' a rod!..." Pinky danced around the apartment, her short skirt flouncing with every pounding step.

All right. She seemed to be in better spirits.

I hid out in the shower. Warm water and a brisk scrub perked me up a bit. As I hooked my bra, I thought fondly of Rae. I put on the same baggy jeans and a fresh white T-shirt. When I got out of the bathroom, the apartment was blissfully quiet. Pinky was hunched over her notebook.

I made a quick call to the Cathedral Hill, but Christa Lovett wasn't answering. We were scheduled to meet that night at six; I wondered if I could sit tight until then.

I said to Pinky, "Ready to go, honey?"

She looked up and grinned. "Yup."

We decided on breakfast in North Beach. As we shuttled downtown on BART, I tried to squelch my nagging anxiety about work and focus on my fashion-plate daughter. Pinky was wearing white stockings, a black mini-skirt dotted with purple dice, a green flannel shirt with a ripped-off collar, a denim jacket, and—the *pièce de résistance*—Day-Glo hair. I smiled as she rattled on about some new trend in free verse.

We were walking under the gloomy shadow of the

TransAmerica building when an open air cable car rolled by on wheels, its handles festooned with a garish "Jordan for Mayor" banner. Loudspeakers blared a patriotic jingle. Campaign workers waved maniacally from inside. I glared at them meanly, but they were undaunted, tooling merrily along to ruin someone else's Saturday morning.

Pinky nudged me. "Don't worry. At least he's not another Maggie Thatcher...."

But I wasn't so sure.

I stopped for a Saturday paper when we turned onto Columbus Avenue. I made Pinky wait while I scanned it. Gold's death had earned a short mention on page three, though somebody else besides Luchetti had nabbed the by-line. Odd. Anyway, I already knew as much as the reporter did. Except for one important tidbit: the foreman's name was Tony Rodriguez. I filed it in my head for future use.

Pinky and I strolled up Columbus, the wide boulevard that dissects North Beach. During the last few decades, the neighborhood had been a haven for beats, punks, and other fringy types. Now, the real counterculture has been largely priced out. North Beach is once again an amalgam of diverse influences: Chinatown butts up against the Italian heart of the city, XXX-rated nightclubs vie with dingy rock clubs, tourists jostle longtime residents, and small businesses struggle—with limited success—to fend off change. Even The Condor, famous for Carol Doda's breasts and the death-by-piano incident, has turned into a bland bistro.

My daughter and I settled at the U.S. Restaurant, an unassuming triangular-shaped place at the juncture of Columbus, Green, and Grant with red-checked tableclothes and generic diner flatware. I defied a Nell Fury tradition and bypassed pasta in favor of plain old scrambled eggs and bacon.

Pinky ordered linguini with clam sauce and extra garlic bread. A chip off the old block.

She still wouldn't talk about Eleven. But that was in the blood, too. I certainly never filled my own mother in on my love life. Now, I thought sadly, I would if I could.

When breakfast was over, I tried Lovett one more time from a pay phone. No luck. Just for the heck of it, I thumbed through the phone book to the Rs. Just as I thought, there were columns full of Rodriguezes, including a bunch of Tonys, Antonios, and Anthonys. I stared at the page for a while, distracted by an unseemly bit of graffiti decorating the left-hand corner.

I pulled out a pen and transformed the rebel artwork into a farm silo with interlocking women's symbols. Then I formulated a plan. But first, one more promised outing with Pinky: Saturday afternoon at the movies.

13

We inadvertently picked a gem, director Nancy Savoca's *Dogfight.* The film was all about first love and the horrors of warfare and the way unrealistic beauty standards traumatize women. I loved the way the serious teenage lead, Lili Taylor, strummed her guitar wistfully and yearned to do something important in life. Then there was the cameo by Holly Near. Sweet.

During the first fumbling sex scene between Taylor and River Phoenix, I heard Pinky sniffling beside me. I watched her surreptitiously. Hmm.

Afterwards, Pinky headed home to rest up for a rave. I was a little nervous about her being out so late, but she reminded me it was a new-fangled kind of event—all peace, love, and flower-power, Nineties style. When it was over, she was staying overnight at a girlfriend's. I made her promise to call me if they needed a ride or something. She said okay.

I made a mental list of my destinations: the Cathedral Hill Hotel, Beaumont Avenue, and 279 Adams Street. I caught a cab for my first stop, then squirmed impatiently in the back when I realized I could have walked just as quickly from the Castro Theatre to Van Ness Avenue. I rolled down the window for a better view of the traffic jam.

Clogging the intersection was a bevy of lights, sandbags, tripods, cameras, full-skirted nuns…good lord! It was a movie production company. A swarm of onlookers gawked from behind flimsy barricades.

I groaned and slouched down in the seat.

The driver muttered, "What the hell?"

Hours later, it seemed, we made it to the door of the Cathedral Hill Hotel.

It was all for naught. No Christa Lovett. No Ms. John Lennon. Nobody who could tell me anything except that Lovett was still checked in. I even kept a look-out for the banana-eyed thug, but he wasn't lurking in any obvious shadows. I took another taxi back to Dolores—a fast trip, thankfully—and retrieved the Mustang. Then I swung a wide detour across town to avoid the pernicious movie-makers. When I got to Beaumont, I parked right in front of the house. This time, I was primed for direct confrontation.

No one was hulking around outside now, but when I rang the bell, a vulture-like apparition loomed in the doorway. He commanded me to state my business. I said I'd do so to any of the Norways. He balked. I balked back. We kept it up for a while until a coifed head of blue-black hair appeared over his right shoulder.

I heard the woman say, "Let it be, Jack. Let me talk to her."

Hooray. Vulture Head grumbled but stepped aside. The

woman who took his place was plump and round-eyed, with bowed pinkish lips and a series of creases ringing her neck. She smiled kindly.

I said: "Are you Mrs. Norway?"

"Oh, heavens, no." Her whole torso shook when she chuckled. "I'm a neighbor, Mrs. Zimmer. And you are—?"

"Nell Fury." I gave her my right hand. She shook it delicately, then gestured me inside.

As we stepped into a side parlor, Mrs. Zimmer said, "The Norways are quite elderly. They're napping now. This has been so hard for them...." She sighed. "I'm just here to...I don't know, help out, I guess. Make sure Rosie's okay. Ellen's a good friend of mine. I just don't understand who would do a thing like this."

"Yes, I'm so sorry."

She looked at me. "Are you a friend of Ellen's, too? Or Philip's?"

"No." I hesitated, then opted for half the truth. "I'm a private investigator. I'm working on a case for Philip's office and"—I nodded conspiratorially—"you know I can't say much about *that*. But my boss wants me to find out what's happening with the ransom request. Of course, the cops won't tell me anything. So...do you know if the exchange is going on tonight as planned?"

Mrs. Zimmer glanced toward the hallway. "Sit down," she whispered. "Let me see what Jack's up to."

She was back in a moment. "He's arguing with Rosie. He'll be back shortly." She sat close to me on the couch. "Listen, all I know is they're planning to do the payoff anyway, despite Philip's death. He and Ellen's parents got the money together, and the police are going to deliver it. It's supposed to be tonight, but I don't know any of the details."

She rolled her round eyeballs.

"Huh." I thought for a second. "Mrs. Zimmer, did you know Philip very well?"

"Ummm, not too well. He just moved in with Ellen about a year ago. She was single when I first met her, but...I don't know. Philip was nice enough."

"So they seemed...in love?"

Mrs. Zimmer smiled at me sadly. "Oh, sure, I guess so. But who knows about these things. Ellen's always been kind of, umm, practical."

She let out a huge sigh and continued, "My god. I wonder if she knows he's dead...."

We sat in mournful silence. I patted Mrs. Zimmer's smooth hand and cast my eyes about the room. Indeed, Ellen Norway appeared to have taste in the practical vein. The small parlor was tidy and comfortably appointed, but rather dull. Even the coffee table magazines were unexciting: *Smithsonian*, *The New Yorker*, some kind of accounting journal. Nothing in the room hinted at her sordid lesbian past.

I got up to check out a photo display on the opposite wall. Philip and Ellen were front and center, holding hands outside the Japanese Tea Garden. The only photo I'd seen of Ellen Norway was a blurry newspaper shot. Here, she looked bright-eyed and efficient in creased culotte shorts and a cardigan sweater. She wore her salt-and-pepper hair shoulder length.

A series of photographs followed Rosie Norway's progress through childhood. She was a good-looking kid, albeit in that blonde cheerleader kind of way. The most recent shot was taken at a beach; Rosie in a wide-legged stance squinting into the camera.

Suddenly, she materialized in the room with Jack the

Vulture hot on her heels. He started to speak, but Mrs. Zimmer butted in. "Rosie, sweetie, this is an old friend of your mom's. Nell...I'm sorry, I've forgotten your last name."

"Fury. Nell Fury." I threw Mrs. Zimmer a grateful glance.

"Yes," Mrs. Zimmer said.

Rosie Norway looked at me indifferently. Like a clod, I said, "How do you do?"

She smiled weakly in response, and an odd sensation tickled the back of my brain. I didn't have time to think about it, though, because Jack blurted, "You're out of here, lady," and everybody started making noise at once.

"That's okay," I said loudly, "I need to leave anyway." I turned to Rosie, "Maybe you'd like to walk down to the corner store with me? Get some fresh air?"

"That'd be great," Mrs. Zimmer enthused, over Jack's protestations. "You haven't been outside since you got home. And pick up some milk, will you dear?"

I hustled Rosie out of there as fast as I could. She seemed a bit shell-shocked, but pleased after all to be away from the Vulture's clutches. I steered her toward Geary Street. She scuffed her laceless Tretorns on the sidewalk and looked at me sideways. "*Who* are you?" she asked, reasonably enough.

"I'm trying to help find your mom," I said quietly. I couldn't keep up the pretense.

She nodded as if that explained everything. Rosie was a few years older than Pinky, but she seemed younger somehow, free of guile and cynicism.

I said: "I'm sorry about Philip's death."

She shrugged.

"You weren't close?"

"No. He was okay. I mean, I'm sorry he died. But —"
Rosie's throat closed up.

"You're worried about your mom?"

She nodded, holding in the tears.

"Yeah, me too." I plunged on recklessly. "But I hear the
ransom is being paid tonight. So you'll see her soon—"

"No, it's tomorrow."

"Really?"

"Mm-hmm." Rosie's ponytail flipped back and forth.
"It was supposed to be tonight, but the guy—the kidnap-
per—changed the plan. It's tomorrow morning."

"Huh. Jack told you that?"

"Well, I overheard him talking. He's the one who's going to do it."

"Did he say what time?"

"No. But early, I think."

"So Jack's a cop?"

Rosie made a horsy noise. "Yeah."

At least she had a healthy teenage disdain for authority.
I asked: "You don't know where it's happening, do you?
The trade-off?"

We stopped for a traffic light. Rosie smiled at me faintly
with thin, whitish lips. "You ask a lot of questions."

The light turned green. Rosie stepped off the curb and finally said, "No, I don't know."

I traipsed after her. There was one more matter I wanted
to discuss, but I couldn't figure out how to broach it. Something was still bugging me about Rosie Norway. I stalled by
asking her about college.

She got teary again. "I just started two weeks ago. I
don't know. Maybe I won't go back. Everything's so
messed up…"

"Why'd you pick Colorado?"

"'Cause I like winter. Snow." She ran her sweatshirt sleeve across her eyes. "But I'm thinking of transferring to Chicago. Maybe Northwestern. I mean, if Mom's okay and everything."

"Chicago?"

"I grew up there," she said matter-of-factly.

Hmmm. I thought Ellen Norway and Christa Lovett had been together in Minneapolis. When Rosie would have been a child. Or maybe Lovett never said where they lived. I stopped suddenly and put a hand on Rosie's shoulder. "What about your father?" I asked. "Is he in Chicago?"

Her face went totally blank. "He died before I was born."

We walked the rest of the way in silence.

I thought about Pinky's dad. As far as I knew, he was very much alive, working at a ranch somewhere in Wyoming. Pinky'd never met him. He took off when I was five months pregnant. Then I met Caroline and we decided to keep the baby. When she was old enough, we told Pinky about her freewheeling father, but so far she'd shown little interest in him. I figured that could change anytime. I had no idea how I'd react if it did.

At the 7-Eleven Rosie bought milk, a Diet Coke, and a packet of Peanut M & M's. I got some Licorice Whips and stashed 'em in my pocket for later. As we headed back, I threw out my final ticklish question.

"Rosie, did you ever know your mom's friend Christa?"

"Uh-uh. But I've heard of her. Mom's got a few pictures of her. Why?"

"So…she never lived with you guys? When you were a kid?"

Rosie looked at me oddly. "No-o-o-o. Why would she?"

"Oh, just wondering."

Damn. Lovett had lied to me again. Unless Rosie was the untruthful one. But that I couldn't picture.

When we got to Beaumont, I gave Rosie a soft hug and wished her the best. Up close, her eyes were sad puddles of pale blue; she seemed desperately alone. I gave her a business card and told her to call me anytime. As she read it, I watched those eyes and felt another weird twinge travel through me. For a regular-enough kid, she sure was spooky.

I made sure Rosie got inside okay. Then I pointed the Mustang back towards town. It was too late to make it to Oakland this afternoon. In fact, I'd better hustle for my six o'clock date with Christa Lovett. I gunned the engine and flew.

14

As it turned out, I needn't have hurried. Christa wasn't in the lobby, nor did she answer when I went and knocked on her hotel room door. Back downstairs, I called from the in-house phone—no response. Damn. I didn't see my rule-defying friend the desk clerk, either.

I sat down on a lumpy plaid sofa in front of a broad plate glass window. Two cabloads of sun-kissed vacationers spilled out and trooped energetically into the lobby. Saturday night in the big sinful city.

I crossed my arms and fumed. Technically, I was done with Christa Lovett. I'd spun my wheels for three days but had kept up my end of the bargain. Now Lovett owed me $400 plus change. I was free to walk out of here.

But my job had odd psychological tentacles that often snared me even when the quest seemed fruitless. I sighed. Get over it, Fury. After all, my own lover and kid were about to leave me in the dust, and here I was obsessing about somebody else's lover and teenage daughter. Hmm. That explains it: pure avoidance.

Then again, I knew I was onto something, and that always gave me a charge. Nobody else was clamoring for my immediate attention. Might as well follow a few more hunches.

I hopped up and made for the bank of phones. I threw two dimes in a slot. Phoebe picked up right away.

I said: "Phoebe Grahame, love of my life."

"Nellie!" Laughter pealed in the backround. "What's the squid?"

"Are you having fun without me?"

"Impossible."

"Humph. Listen, what time's the show tonight?"

Phoebe yelled for the revelers to shut up. Then she said to me: "Nine o'clock. But can you come over for dinner? We're just starting to cook."

I said no thanks. Three hours would give me plenty of time to get to Oakland and back.

I told Phoebe I'd meet them at Josie's Cabaret. Phoebe's lover, Johnnie Blue, was a stand-up comic. She was performing tonight at a benefit to raise money for a group organizing against media censorship, in the aftermath of the Gulf War and beyond. Along with Johnnie, I'd get to see the hilarious Marga Gomez, the outlandish Elvis Herselvis, an up-and-coming musical duo named Les & Jan, and others. Of all the performers, I'd heard Les & Jan were especially hot—kind of like the Indigo Girls, only cuter and with more personality.

After wishing Phoebe *bon appétit*, I replaced the receiver. Then I dug out my little black book. When I worked for Continent West, I compiled a list of congenial colleagues around the country who scratched each other's backs from time to time. I decided there was no need to bother my Brooklyn contact. Instead, I found the name of a woman in the Windy City who I'd once assisted. Time to call in a favor.

When she answered the phone, I realized I'd interrupted another person's Saturday night. I heard the sexy strains of saxophone coming over the wire and the slurred speech of Rochelle Lamb. I knew Rochelle hit the sauce. But I also knew—on Tad Greenblatt's good word—that she was one of the best PIs in the business. Rochelle was a Black woman in her fifties, an ex-cop who had spent time in prison for dipping into the evidence. She had defied the odds by straightening up inside. Once sprung, she'd turned her vast experience into a lucrative, and mostly aboveboard, livelihood.

"Rochelle? It's Nell Fury, from San Francisco."

"Nellll." She strung out my name and burped. "How's it goin'?"

"Fine. Shall I call back another time? Tomorrow?"

"Nah. What'd ya need, hon?"

"A favor."

I asked Rochelle to check county birth records for one Rosie Norway, possibly Rose, Rosemary or Roseanne. Since I figured her between 17 and 19, I suggested she try from 1972 to 1974. I said the mother's name was Ellen Norway. Since the baby may have been tagged with the father's surname, I asked Rochelle to keep an eye out for any little Roses.

Rochelle snickered into the phone.

I asked her to search in Cook County. Then I remembered Ellen Norway's wealth and asked her to try Lake

County, too, just in case.

Rochelle mumbled something about a needle in a haystack. But she said, "Okey-doke, honey. First thing Monday. You can count on old Rochelle...." She pronounced it "Roach Hell."

"Thanks," I said.

"Chicago misses you, Nell baby. Come on out and see me sometime...." She hung up before I had a chance to respond.

I shook my head and turned for the exit. Ms. John Lennon fell into step beside me. I jumped.

"Hi," she said softly. Then she handed me a small envelope with the hotel insignia in the upper left corner.

I started to speak but she broke in. "The woman in 317 left this at the desk. For you. I mean—" She rotated her shaggy head and carefully scouted our surroundings. "I mean, I figured out it was you. She said you'd be here at six."

"When did you talk to her?"

"This morning," she whispered. Her eyes shone rather feverishly. "Around 9 a.m."

"Did she check out?!" I stammered.

"No." Another furtive glance. "She's here. She's paid up through Wednesday."

Ms. Lennon sidled away and disappeared through a door marked "Private." She reappeared a moment later behind the counter, looking pleased with herself.

What a character, I thought, as I ran a finger along the edge of the envelope. But at least she got the job done. When it was time to foment revolution, I'd be sure and recruit her into the fold.

I lifted the flap and drew out a single piece of hotel stationery. Lovett had left me a note and a cashier's check for $500. She thanked me for my efforts and said there was nothing more for me to do. She'd call to say goodbye before leaving town.

At least I thought that's what she said. Her handwriting was one continuous scrawl, like an almost flat line tracing the heartbeat of a dying patient.

I strolled to the desk and saddled the clerk with one more responsibility. I gave her a business card and asked her to call me if Christa Lovett acted weird or checked out or did anything else out of the ordinary. Ms. John Lennon's bright eyes registered no change of emotion. She slipped the card into the front pocket of her uniform and turned to greet a paying customer.

15

I turned to KNBR radio 680 as I steered the Mustang toward the entrance to the San Francisco-Oakland Bay Bridge. The Giants and the Cubs were in the midst of a twilight game out at Candlestick Park. It was the top of the fifth and the Cubs were up 2–1. Amazing.

I listened to the buzz of the crowd and the lulling drone of Hank and Ron, and waited patiently for an actual burst of activity on the field. I wished I had a pack of peanuts and a malted. As a consolation prize, I scrounged the Licorice Whips out of my pocket and ripped into the cellophane. I chewed slowly and maneuvered the car onto the on-ramp.

Traffic flowed steadily on the lower deck of the bridge. By the time I passed Treasure Island, the Giants had jumped ahead 3-2. I clicked off the dial and listened to the hum of the wheels as they rolled over the roadway, their smooth passage marred only by the occasional seam running perpendicularly across the bridge.

I finished the licorice and tossed the wrapper into the back seat. As I eyeballed the traffic signs at the far side of the bridge, I thought, yet again, about getting a pair of glasses. I squinted and followed the signs. I was roughly familiar with parts of Oakland, but I still relied on maps and road markers to get around.

Nightfall was coming on as I exited onto Grand Avenue and cruised by the eastern tip of the lake. It felt peaceful over here, at least compared to frenetic old Frisco. Of course, Oakland is a big town, with a rhythm and a set of attributes and problems that I—as an outsider—couldn't begin to understand.

During my infrequent visits, I'd experienced Oakland as a city of contrasts, like most urban outposts in the segregated United States. Some areas, with their wide white avenues and dried-out patches of grass, reminded me of Los Angeles. Other sections seemed like Roxbury, Massachusetts— weather-beaten shacks, long rows of boarded-up commercial properties, legions of unemployed people passing time on street corners.

But here, north of Lake Merritt, the city had a sleepy Midwestern feel. Old-fashioned businesses lined the main boulevards. Stately apartment buildings snaked up side streets, flanked by greenery and the bright splash of flowers. Over by the lake, people recreated in the warm September dusk. A ring of twinkly lights circled Lake Merritt, casting a warm glow as inviting as a cakeful of birthday candles.

I pulled over to check my map. Adams was up a hill, off Lee Street. I drove forward, turned right, and followed Lee for several blocks. I hung another right on Adams and rolled slowly by number 279. It was a squat stucco building painted blue, its three-sided horseshoe design surrounding a modest fountain in the center. Lights shone over four doorways along the inside of the horseshoe. The handsome building was well-shielded by healthy shrubbery and vivid bougainvillaea. I didn't see any action in or near the apartment house. I parked behind a Datsun B210 and strode back on foot.

I had no idea which unit housed Sue Ann Paige, so I halted by the row of mailboxes positioned near the front walk. I scanned the names: no Paige. Then I did a double-take. The plastic strip below box #4 read Myles.

Myles…Myles…shit! The rangy receptionist at Ellen Norway's accounting firm was named Tucker Myles. I let out a nervous chuckle. Myles was a common enough name. Still…

Quickly, I walked towards apartment #4 and punched the bell. No one appeared. I knocked loudly; still no response. I gave the door handle a twist. Sure enough, it was locked up tight, and the only windows fronting the building were firmly draped shut.

I waited a few more minutes, but nothing happened. I looked around the courtyard. There wasn't a soul around, either here or outside the other buildings up and down the block. I sallied on over to #3. Again, I found no one home. Next I tried #2. The mailbox had told me someone named Shardlow lived here. Perhaps that's who opened the door and spat out, "Yeah? Whadda ya want?"

"Excuse me, sir," I said, "I was looking for Sue Ann Paige, and I—"

"She's out of town."

"Pardon?"

He heaved with exasperation. "Lady, I said she was out of town."

"You mean, she's on vacation?"

"No!" he thundered, then paused to take some shallow breaths.

Geez, buddy, watch that blood pressure.

Shardlow mustered up an artificial calm and continued, "She's a teacher. She went on sabbatical. Whaddaya want with her?"

I ignored the question. "Oh, I see. So is the apartment vacant?"

He sighed, hugely. "If you're here about the sublet, it's already taken." He started to close the door, but I thrust my foot in its path.

"Hang on a sec," I said. "Who sublet the place?"

I thought Shardlow might pop a seam. He seethed, "I-don't-know-who-lives-there. Now move your goddamn foot."

"Tall woman? Copper-colored hair?"

"Yup, that sounds like it," he growled.

I pulled back my foot. "Sorry to bother you," I lied, then turned to sprint across the courtyard.

I listened to another blasphemy and the slamming of the door. I couldn't help but smile. Back outside #4, I paused to think. Somehow, Tucker Myles' phone number ended up in the dirt at the Budget Barn construction site. Well, Philip Gold surely knew her as a co-worker of Ellen's. So why was he carrying around her number? Unless, for some reason, the foreman Tony Rodriguez had dropped the slip of paper. Either way, I couldn't fit the puzzle pieces together.

I looked up at the cobalt sky. Wow, you could actually see faint stars from this side of the bay. I pondered my options. I couldn't break in through the front door; the apartment was too visible. So I could await Tucker Myles' return.

Or I could come back later. Or I could scout the back of the building for possible ways to get inside.

I chose the latter option. I walked around one end of the horseshoe. It was pretty dark now, but I spotted a narrow dirt path winding down between chest-high bushes. A few paces later I was completely hidden by the tangle of shrubbery. The path opened out a bit, and I realized I was right alongside the back wall of Myles' unit. I pulled out my pen light and pointed it at the stucco wall.

There was no back door, but there were a couple of windows covered by flimsy screens. If I could dislodge the mesh, I bet I could jimmy one of the window sashes. I stepped closer, through the brush, to check it out. My foot rammed into something solid. Damn. I couldn't see through the bramble, but I could tell an obstacle was blocking my access to the windows. I shown the light downward.

And then I felt a gorge rise up that sent me reeling, flailing against the branches, choking on a terror that forced my breath to come in shallow, ragged gulps. I stumbled and dropped to all fours, heaving dry sobs into the dusty earth. I made myself look again. In the dim yellow glow of the pen light, I saw somebody lying face down, one arm twisted awkwardly back, the other wedged against the base of the wall. The figure wore snug jeans and a short flight jacket. The head was angled sideways, a mat of tangled hair obscuring the face.

I cried silently as I bent forward to sweep aside the hair. A large clot of crusty black blood obscured the right temple. But I saw faint movement in one eyelid and two ragged lips struggling to suck in air. Oh, god, this was no stranger. As I leaned over to embrace the ravaged form, I wailed out loud, so loudly, in fact, that all of Oakland and maybe the world could hear the wretched sound.

Lydia Luchetti—ace reporter, determined politico, devoted feminist and irksome friend—had been in the wrong place one too many times.

16

I never made it to the anti-censorship benefit. The only show I was privy to that night was the spectacle of Oakland law enforcement running roughshod over the scene of the crime—and over my emotions.

I didn't call 911 myself. A neighbor heard my cry of distress by the time I raced around to the front of 279 Adams, a couple of uniforms were roaring up in a blaze of light and commotion. An ambulance arrived minutes later and whisked Lydia away to the emergency room. She was unconscious; they said it'd be touch-and-go.

For the ensuing two and a half hours, I chatted with the cops, answering and reanswering the same questions. Fortunately, I had collected myself well enough by then to respond level-headedly.

I told them I was on a case. And that I'd found Tucker Myles' phone number at the site of Philip Gold's murder in San Francisco. Yes, there must be some connection between that murder and this shooting. I also admitted that I knew Lydia Luchetti. But I said—quite truthfully—that I didn't know what she was doing at Myles' residence in Oakland. I continued to keep my mouth shut about Christa Lovett.

During the course of the evening, I learned that no handgun was recovered, either in or outside the apartment. But a cartridge casing from a semiautomatic was found in the dirt. There were no immediate suspects, though Tucker Myles could not be located. The last known person to speak with Lydia before the assault was a *Chronicle* editor, who phoned her last night about three o'clock. Except for me, of course, whom she called soon thereafter.

At some point during the long ordeal, we left the crime scene to the technicians and ga-ga-eyed neighbors and trundled down to headquarters. Once there, I excused myself to call the hospital. No word yet, but Lydia was still alive. I went to use the bathroom. The dingy lavatory smelled vaguely of puke and disinfectant, but the cool, quiet solitude was a balm on my nerves. I sunk back against the pale green tiles and rested on my heels. I was all cried out.

I caught my reflection in the distorted plane of a full-length mirror. Under the cruel glare of fluorescent lights, my face was green and puffy, my chestnut hair a fright wig of mammoth proportions. My jacket was ripped and dirty. I realized with a jolt that my palms were torn and crusty with blood. I must have scraped them in my frenzied fall back at the apartment building.

I got up to rinse them and felt the sting as water ran over the ragged gashes. Ugly. I patted them down with scratchy brown paper towels and went to use the toilet. Afterwards, I spent a few minutes stretching my exhausted limbs. Then I left my private haven and reentered the hectic corridors of the Oakland PD.

Somebody had already called Luchetti's family in Ne-braska. A sister was flying west immediately. I asked about Lydia's lover. Yeah, she'd been informed, too, and was on her way to the hospital. The sergeant who told me that sneered as he said it. Shit. Even though I'd never been fond of Lydia's lover, Margaret Halliway, my heart leapt in her defense. If Lydia died, she'd experience enough agony as it was without having to deal with the cruelties of a hostile world. Halliway was a tough cookie, though, and used to public scrutiny. She was the San Francisco District Attorney and had finally come out of the closet within the last year.

The head honcho told me I could go. Great—my car was still parked on Adams Street. I felt like company, anyway, so I tried reaching Phoebe. She was still out. No answer at Rae's, either. When I punched Tad Greenblatt's number, he picked up with a lazy, "Hellllo?"

"Tad-o, it's me."

"Hey. Fury."

"Hey. What're you doing?"

"Watching *L.A. Law*. A re-run."

"*L.A. Law*?!" I'd pegged Tad as a strict junkie for sports and Arsenio Hall.

"Yup," he said, "I've got a crush on C.J."

"Don't we all!"

It felt good to laugh. Then I told Tad what was going on and asked him to come over and pick me up. He said he was on the way.

It was 11:15 p.m. when Tad arrived to squire me from downtown Oakland to my stranded vehicle. I kicked myself when we got there. I'd parked right behind Lydia's beat-up old Datsun and hadn't even recognized it. Not that it would have helped. I pointed the car out to one of the cops still hovering around and turned to leave.

Tad told me to follow him. His taillights guided me through a maze of hushed streets. After a while Tad rolled across traffic and stopped in the parking lot of Dave's, a 24-hour restaurant on Broadway. Suddenly, I was famished.

"How'd you know?!" I beamed, as we strolled to the entrance.

"Fury, is the Pope Catholic?"

"Verrry original," I drawled, and socked old Greenblatt in the shoulder.

An hour later, Tad had his paw around a Chesterfield, and I was inhaling second-hand smoke. I'd downed a turkey club, a mound of rippled potato chips, and a dill pickle. I couldn't remember what Tad had eaten. I slurped the dregs of my Coke and said, "You know what the last thing Lydia said to me was?"

"What?"

"She said, 'You owe me one.'"

"Nellie. She might be okay. Don't get maudlin."

"Oh, I'm not." I sighed. "It's just...I really do owe her one, you know? I really need to figure this out."

"Why? You pay your taxes. Let them handle it."

God. He could be so infuriating. I changed tacks. "I think Tucker Myles has vanished. I wonder if she found out something about the kidnapping—"

"Either that or she's *in* on the kidnapping."

"Huh."

"What's her story, anyway?"

I explained that Myles worked in Ellen Norway's office. I described her lanky, polished appearance and told Tad about the chilly reception I got from her and the CPA.

He asked, "You think she's a dyke?"

"Myles?"

"Yeah."

"I don't know. I never thought about it." I paused. "You think she and—"

"Uh-huh. What if she and Norway 'have a thing goin' on...'" Tad burst into song.

Yeah. What if they did? What if Ellen Norway was still a lesbian, and had planned to marry Philip Gold strictly for convenience? And...what if Christa Lovett found out about Tucker Myles? Was her jealousy potent enough to fuel murder?

I laughed.

"What's so funny?" Tad stabbed out his cigarette.

"I've got this scenario going in my head that's as wild as the plot of *Fatal Attraction*."

"Yeah?" Tad grinned. "Wanna write a screenplay? We could get out of this shithole profession, go live up in Pacific Heights with Danielle Steel..."

"Dream on, Greenblatt."

Tad offered to see me home, but I said no, thanks. I sprung for the meal, then hugged him goodbye in the parking lot. I was still bone-weary and traumatized somewhere inside, but my thoughts were now racing, my body wired up. I flew home across the upper span of the bridge, watching the beam of the Alcatraz lighthouse sweep an eerie arc over the wide murky waters of the San Francisco Bay.

17

I paralleled into a tiny slot between a VW bug and an Olds as big as a motorboat. Ramona Avenue looked almost tranquil under the moonlit sky, with its sprinkling of acacia trees and shuttered bay windows hanging sleepily over the garages. I don't know why it's called an avenue, anyway; Ramona is just a narrow, one-way block tucked unobtrusively into one corner of the North Mission.

But it's *my* avenue, I thought contentedly, as I readied my keys between my knuckles for the short walk to my apartment door. Halfway there, I froze. A figure sat huddled in the shadows of the entranceway. He started to rise and I took a step back, thinking fast, ready to turn and flee if necessary.

"Wait," he said. His command was quiet but tense.

I held my pose, keys gripped firmly in my fist, and tried to place the voice. I couldn't do it. I rolled up on the balls of my feet, then down, staying loose.

The man stepped forward. I finally got a look at his face and let out an even breath I didn't know I'd been holding. He was a husky fellow dressed to kill in a double-breasted suit that looked gray in the muted light. Henry Gravatt, the CPA from Norway's firm.

I spoke calmly. "It's late. What are you doing here?"

"Listen," he said, still quiet. "We need to talk." He showed me both palms. "I didn't mean to frighten you, ma'am. Really. I'm Henry Gravatt, from—"

"Yeah, I know who you are. How do you know who *I* am?"

"Tucker threw your business card in the trash. I dug it out. Look—" He hitched his trousers. "Let's start over. I just want to talk. I've been waiting here for hours."

I dropped my keys in my pocket and shook out my sweaty palm. Now I recognized his voice, too—this was the guy who'd left the truncated message on my answering machine. I looked hard at Gravatt. His tie was loosened and his suit, on closer inspection, was creased with wrinkles. His eyes were grave, the lids heavy. I almost smiled. "Just how long were you going to wait here, Mr. Gravatt?"

He torqued his head from side to side. "Damn, I don't know. As long as I had to."

"Okay." I walked forward. "You're right, we need to talk. In fact, I was going to look you up tomorrow. So how about we call it a night—"

"No." The tension was back in his voice.

"All right, all right." I trusted him, but not enough to invite him inside. I gestured him back to the entranceway. "So here we are. Let's talk."

We sat together on the cold, hard stoop. Gravatt drew out a pack of Marlboros. I borrowed one, just to hold it between my fingers. I watched the glow at the end of his cigarette, a lovely orange flare that reminded me of dancing and sticky floors and barstools and long nights not unlike this one. Only then, nobody was telling me about extortion plans.

"...so I think Tucker's with Ellen," he summarized, cocking his head to light another Marlboro.

I said: "Shit."

According to Henry Gravatt, CPA, things hadn't been the same at the office since Tucker Myles started working there as office manager five months ago. He didn't like her from the start, but he figured it was just a personality clash. Then she started giving him the creeps. I thought that was funny, considering that Gravatt was the size of your average middle linebacker. But then, the intricacies of office dynamics can buffalo anyone who's just trying to get a job done.

"The creeps, how?" I asked.

"Ohhh, she always comes early and stays late. It's like she's watching me all the time, or something. She keeps the books, does the payroll — I started thinking she was planning some scam." He flipped his hand. "She's a smart bird."

"What about your partners? Did you talk to them about it?"

"Nope. Joey's away on paternity leave. It's just me and Ellen and—" He loosened his tie even further. "Shit. Ellen and Tucker, you know..."

Gravatt couldn't think of the words. I helped him out: "They're having an affair?"

"Shit, yeah."

I smiled. Chalk one up to Greenblatt. I rolled the cigarette between my palms and said, "Okay. So—is it common knowledge? The affair?"

"No. Uh-uh. Ellen was marrying that guy, Gold. No,

they were careful about it, but…you know, I was around, I saw things."

"Henry," I said judiciously, "what if Tucker Myles gives you 'the creeps' simply because she's nervous? She's in the closet, she's having an affair, she's working hard at a new job—"

Gravatt broke in. "Man, you're ready to give the lady all kinds of credit."

"Umm. But you have no proof, right? Of this supposed extortion or embezzlement or whatever?"

"No. I've checked all the on-line data, all the files. I can't find any discrepancies." He shrugged.

"So why'd you come to me?"

"Ellen's supposedly kidnapped and Gold's dead—something is screwed up. I thought a private eye could, I don't know, do something."

I smiled—what a vote of confidence. Then I asked, "But why not just go to the police?"

Gravatt's stern eyes looked straight at me. "No cops. No way."

Geez. First Lovett, now him. The SFPD was certainly anathema these days. I must have looked puzzled because Gravatt said, "Look, I just can't do it. I've got a history, you understand?"

Yeah, I understood. And then, in a flash, I had a "Eureka!" experience, like old Archimedes had when he jumped into the bathtub. Christa Lovett must have a history, too.

I asked Gravatt what he wanted me to do. Check out Myles, he said. Find Norway. And find out if they were ripping off the firm, or planning to.

Suddenly, I had another paying client. I told Gravatt my terms and we were off and running. We agreed to exchange the deposit and contract another time. Then I had a superhuman burst of adrenalin—I asked Gravatt to take me downtown to his office, right now.

He balked. "I don't know, Nell, what about the security guard—"

"You work there, right? Tell 'em you have some late-night business."

He took a hard drag of tobacco. "Yeah, me coming in at night, with a white lady…"

Hmm. I met Gravatt's eyes. And thought about how I muscle my way through everything, go anywhere I want, and rarely think about it twice. Not everyone has that kind of access. I smiled sadly and turned to gaze up and down the tree-studded street.

I said softly, "Let's do it anyway, Henry. Tell 'em I'm a client, with an accounting emergency."

Gravatt laughed loud and hard. But he finally assented.

We took the Mustang, Gravatt riding shotgun, me telling him about the assault outside Tucker Myles' apartment. I got all choked up again. My companion got quiet. The night guard down on Sansome Street seemed only slightly nonplussed by our 2 a.m. visit. Henry Gravatt showed me around, then I spent close to an hour combing Myles' desk and not-so-secret personnel file.

The latter gave her previous job as administrative assistant at Levi Strauss. Her age: 32. Education: B.A. from a college I'd never heard of in Kansas City. Address: Clay Street in San Francisco's upper Fillmore. Huh. Why had she taken the sublet in Oakland?

At first, Myles' desk seemed to offer up nothing. But when I pawed through a drawer full of miscellanea, I found a Julie's Supper Club matchbook with a name and number inked on the inside flap. Tony. I'll be darned. Tony Rodriguez of the orange hard hat? The foreman who found Gold's body?

I memorized the phone number and returned the matchbook to its drawer.

It was 3:15 a.m. by the time I chauffeured Henry to his car, reparked the convertible, and dragged myself upstairs. No Pinky. In a way, I was glad she was staying at her friend's house after kicking up her heels all night with the smart drink crowd. I didn't want to tell her about another assault, another possible tragedy, another wrinkle in my vexing investigation. Plus, I didn't want her to see me looking like hell.

I took a long bath, letting my skin pucker in the warm pool of water. I brushed my teeth. I carefully cleaned my sliced palms with hydrogen peroxide. Then I went to bed straight away, forgetting to feed the fish and ignoring the insistent green blink of the phone machine that told me three callers wanted the attention of Nell Fury, Private Eye.

18

My square-faced clock told me it was 11 a.m. I fought to pull myself to a seated position, and blinked against the bright light penetrating the attic window. Whew. I felt like I'd gone ten rounds with George Foreman.

I stepped to the floor and wandered towards the front room. Flannery and Carson were bobbing at the top of the bowl, giving me the evil eye. I grinned, tossed in some fish flakes, and went to start the coffee. On my way to the bathroom, I looked in on Pinky.

She was home all right, her pink locks outlined against the pillow like the sprouty head of a Lisa Simpson doll. Slumbering noiselessly next to her was another figure. I gaped and looked closer. The head had dark hair and a minor complexion problem. It was Eleven.

Shit. I stumbled into the kitchenette and poured a cup of joe. I gripped my mug and stared into Emma Goldman's eyes. *She* would've approved. Did I? No. Did I have a different set of standards for Pinky than for myself and Red Emma? Yeah, but Pinky was just a kid....

I sighed and let the first sip of coffee slide down my throat. When I was fifteen, I was already fumbling around with young women in movie theaters and vacant lots. I ran with a whole crowd who came of age that way. We learned the tricks with one another, clinging fiercely to the secret thrill of illicit love. But we'd never have brought our girl-friends home to our mothers.

So maybe that was a good thing: Pinky felt comfortable enough to bring the guy home. Of course, she was engaging in garden variety heterosexuality, nothing to shock the troops. Damn, I was hopelessly confused.

I poured a second cup and called the hospital. Lydia was still in critical condition but had made it through surgery. A nurse told me they'd removed a slug from her skull; it was too early to tell about possible brain damage. And Luchetti hadn't yet been able to name her assailant or explain what had happened. I sighed heavily, then asked if Meg Halli-way—Lydia's lover—was around. Nope, she'd gone home to rest. I'd have to reach her later.

I wandered downstairs to fetch the Sunday paper and sat outside for a while in the coolish breeze, watching a father-daughter duo toss around the pigskin. Then I smudged my fingers with newsprint. Nothing much in the Pink section—though I made a mental list of all the movies I was missing. I especially wanted to see a sure-to-be-sappy love story, *My Heroes Have Always Been Cowboys*. And a French film called *Love Without Pity*. Indeed.

When I got to the Sunday magazine section I read the cover story intently. It was another rundown on the struggles of the San Francisco Arts Commission, including the debate about broadening the city's arts advocacy board and the latest word on supposed mismanagement of funds. The article accused the Commission of dragging its feet on the promised internal audit. It also gave prominent attention to freedom of expression activists, including members of the group whose benefit I'd missed last night. They charged the Commission with, in a word, wimpiness.

The magazine had been printed before Philip Gold's death, as a sensitive insert explained. Still, it was unsettling to read Gold's quotations defending and extolling the Arts Commission. Other quoted supporters included the mayor, City Supervisor Jed Flack, Gold's co-chair on the civic design review committee, Stan Raphaelson, and Louise Wong, the outgoing president of the commission.

Suddenly I remembered I'd never heard back from the Commission's staff accountant. Then I had another flash of insight. I'd been assuming Gold's murder had something to do with the kidnapping, or perhaps his shady dealings with old Hard Hat. But maybe not. Maybe Gold's demise was related to the Arts Commission—to his involvement with misappropriation of monies owed to multicultural art and theater groups.

God, Fury. Another Hollywood blockbuster fantasy. I almost laughed aloud imagining a pack of painters and actors ganging up on Gold, with First Amendment absolutists joining in to put a new spin on the meaning of free expression.

Some time later, I retreated upstairs to get a move on things. I glanced furtively at the futon. The kids were still snoozing.

I rummaged through my clean clothes, finally pulling on the smoke-hued sweater over loose-fitting light gray trousers. I tied on white hightop Keds. Kind of sporty. Then I went back to the front room, turned the machine to low volume, and listened to yesterday's phone messages.

Phoebe was first. She was worried when I didn't show up last night at Josie's. Then Rosie Norway: the ransom exchange had been called off again. She wanted to hire me to find her mom. Jesus, when it rains. The third caller was Princess, the amazon camerawoman. Hmm.

I started dialing. Phoebe wasn't in but I left her a reassuring message. I knew she was out at the racetrack indulging her passion for the ponies. I called Rae and tried to finagle a date with her. She couldn't do it that night, so we settled on Monday. I told Rae about Lydia Luchetti, too, and we talked for a while. It helped.

Next, I tried to reach Inspector Peter Little. He was off duty, but another homicide hack gave me the run-around when I told him my name. He would only say that Philip Gold's case was still open, way open. He wouldn't tell me anything about the foreman, Rodriguez. Or about the Ellen Norway snatch, either.

I replaced the receiver, doodling little mini-hard hats on a notepad as I considered my next move. I snagged the receiver once more and punched Rosie's number.

Her voice came on in a hurried rush. "Hello?"

"Rosie? Hi, it's Nell Fury."

"Oh," she stammered.

"I got your message. I wanted to talk about—"

"Never mind."

"What?"

Rosie blustered, "I mean, it's okay. I don't need your

help after all."

"But"—I struggled to comprehend—"what's going on? Is your mom back?!"

"Oh. Oh no. But…the cops…I think they can handle it—"

"Rosie," I said firmly, "that's not what you said in the message. You said—"

"I know!" Rosie Norway sounded frantic. "I know, but I was wrong. Everything's fine!"

I tried to calm her down. "Look, Rosie, I can come visit you if you want. And I *can* help you. If it's the money—"

"No," she twirped. "I'm going to hang up. Forget I called." Click.

I looked at the mouthpiece, then slowly lowered it into place. Something was very funky here. Lovett was avoiding me; now so was Rosie Norway. Had Lovett contacted her? Had her mother?

I wondered—again—about Ellen Norway's kidnapping. Was it a sham? Were she and Tucker Myles at large somewhere, doing…something?

I etched a stick figure, tall and lean, with a cap of shoulder-length hair on top. Then I remembered another tall woman. I picked up the phone again and placed a call.

Princess Diana answered, "Good afternoon. It's second and seven, Young is back to pass—"

"Ah, hello?" I said.

"And it's overrrrrr Rice's shoulder! Damn. Hello?"

"Uh." I laughed nervously. "Is that Princess? This is Nell Fury."

"Nell," she purred. "What do you think of Young?"

"Who's Young?"

"*Steve* Young! Montana's back-up."

"Oh, sorry. I don't know—"

"Ohhhhh." Princess emitted an exaggerated sigh. "You don't like the 9ers."

"Well, it's not the 49ers so much, it's just football—"

"Ahhhh, no!" Now she really played up the mournful routine. I laughed. Princess continued, "Not to worry. We'll work around our differences."

"I beg your pardon?"

"I can love all kinds," she whispered lustily.

Oh, my god. I thought she'd called about the Gold murder. I said, "That's very big of you."

"Hmm. Hang on." I heard TV commotion in the background. Princess said, "They have to punt. So...what are you doing tonight?"

"I don't know," I said honestly.

"How about dinner *chez* Bafaloukos?"

I smiled. "Your name is Princess Bafaloukos?"

"That's me, Greek-Armenian and Norwegian on my mother's side. You should hear my full name."

"Maybe after we know each other better," I flirted back. Yikes—where did that come from?

"Thatta girl," Princess said. "How about eight?"

I said okay and wrote down the address. We rang off. I was shaking my head dumbfoundedly when Pinky shuffled by, her Pebble Beach sweatshirt hanging to her knees. She gasped when she saw me. "Mum..."

"Hi, sweetie." I kissed her on the forehead.

Pinky looked wildly from side to side, the flush in her cheeks rising to match her hair color.

"Pink, I know he's here."

She peered at me. I could read both anger and humiliation in her eyes. She said slowly, "I thought you'd be out. You said you were going to the ball game."

126

"Oh." She was right. "I canceled. I saw Tad last night and...other things have come up."

Pinky stared down at her feet.

I said: "Go ahead with your shower, honey. I'll make some fresh coffee."

While she was in the bathroom, Eleven wandered out and practically broke into a sweat when he saw me. I loved it— Eleven, the motor-mouth, stunned into silence. He reconnoitered with Pinky, then beat a hasty path out the front door.

Fifteen minutes later, Pinky emerged with wet hair, red eyes and a ravenous appetite. I'd assembled a tray of fresh fruit and English muffins. We sat at the counter and munched quietly for a while. Finally, I broke into a song-and-dance about birth control and safer sex.

Pinky interrupted me. "Mum, I know. You've told me all this. And Caroline has too. Jesus."

I looked at her steadily. "Okay, you know it. Are you practicing it?"

Pinky turned her head. She'd put her sweatshirt back on, and now she pulled down the sleeves, hid her hands, and crossed her arms over her chest. She didn't answer.

I sighed. "Pinky, there's nothing wrong with...intimacy...it's just...I just want you to be happy!" I blurted, sounding like every mother everywhere who wanted something intangible for which there was no guarantee.

Both of us got a little choked up. Pinky mumbled, "We didn't do anything...."

I looked at her, startled.

She went on, "He just came over to sleep. I ran into him last night and we all stayed over at Gina's. But, you know, we were still tired...." Pinky stood and wandered over to the stove. She started fiddling with the dials.

"Oh," I said carefully, hiding my relief. "Oh."

Pinky's back was still turned. I picked up a pear and took a bite. The silence seemed to linger for hours. I finished the pear and started in on an apple. Then Pinky came over and sat back down, a measure of the old sauciness in evidence on her face.

"How was the rave?" I asked.

"Bitchin'," Pinky said, with just a touch of a tease in her voice.

"I'm sorry I missed it." I reached over and hugged her hard.

"Mum, you know, I'm leaving in two days."

"I know, sweetie." Actually, I'd sort of blocked it out. And Rae's departure, too.

Pinky said: "I'll miss you."

"Yeah, me too...."

It was two o'clock by the time we cleaned up and figured out the next 48 hours. Today, Pinky was off to see another one of her friends. So we blocked out some time for tomorrow. Then she went to get dressed. When she kissed me goodbye, leaving a smear of pink lipstick on my cheek, I realized I'd probably never know what went wrong between her and Eleven—and what made it all right again.

19

"¿Hola?" a woman's voice answered.

"Hola, ¿cóma...cómo está?" I stumbled, kicking myself once again for screwing around during Spanish class. I muddled on. *"¿Tony? ¿Es Tony en casa?"*

"Un momento."

I heard the phone clunk down, then a racket in the background that sounded an awful lot like the same old 49ers game. A man came on the line.

"Hola," I repeated. "Tony Rodriguez?"

"Sí."

Touché. The phone number on Tucker Myles' matchbook belonged to Tony Rodriguez, the man in the orange hard hat. I said, *"¿Habla ingles?"*

"Yes," he said with annoyance.

"Mr. Rodriguez, my name is Nell Fury. I'd like to speak with you about Philip Gold. I—"

"I already squared it with you people," he said, and started to hang up.

"Wait! I'm not a cop." I sensed his hesitation and fibbed, "I'm working with the family of Ellen Norway. You know, Gold's fiancée? I just want to hear your side of what happened that night."

No response.

"Mr. Rodriguez?"

He seethed: "I told you, I already talked to the police. I don't owe nobody nothing. *Nada.*"

Hmm. Hardball time. "Look, I understand that. As I said, I'm not a cop. But you see—" I paused. "I happen to know you and Gold had a conversation that day. The day he died."

I listened to Rodriguez breathe in and out. I twirled the phone cord around my finger and waited. Eventually he said, "And how do you happen to know that, miss?"

"I was there."

"*¿Es verdad?* You were there?" He grunted. "Now, who did you say you were?"

I repeated my name. And explained I was a private investigator.

"Miss," Rodriguez said evenly. "So I talked to Gold? He worked for the city—we did business. Big deal. All the guys saw us."

"Yeah, but did they all see him slip you a manila envelope?"

Again, the even breathing. When Rodriguez spoke again, his voice was edgy. "Just what do you want?"

"To talk. I want to know what Gold was doing down there at the site. What you know about the murder."

Rodriguez consented, but I could tell he wasn't too happy about it. He suggested we meet on Twenty-fourth Street.

I was surprised when he named the spot: the St. Francis Fountain, an old-time soda shop a bit out of synch with the rest of the neighborhood. Of course, the St. Francis was the lunch counter of choice for the founders of the 49ers footfall franchise, back in the 1940s. Maybe all the tough guys hung out there.

What the heck. I said sure. We agreed on a time and hung up simultaneously.

I cranked open the convertible for the short spin through the Mission. My car is nothing compared to some of the vintage clunkers roaming the local streets—long gold Cadillacs, shiny low-riding Lincolns, jacked-up monstrosities hogging two lanes of traffic. I made a detour to the bank to deposit the check from Christa Lovett. Then I headed for Twenty-fourth Street.

I wanted to park some distance away from our meeting spot. Finding a vacant bit of curb near the corner of Twenty-fifth and Florida, I pulled in and closed up the car. I ran a hand along the side of the powder-blue flivver and set off on foot.

The sun was a steady friend here in the heart of the Mission. I felt sweat collect beneath my sweater as I dodged clumps of children, women with strollers, and garage-sale paraphernalia that littered the sidewalk in random patches. Things were even livelier on Twenty-fourth Street: bustling produce stands, teenage skateboarders, the pulse of mariachi music coursing out the open door of a neighborhood bar. I passed the artfully spare exhibit space of the Galleria de la Raza. One block down, I stopped to survey the St. Francis

Fountain storefront, a mosaic of black-and-white tiles with neon Deco lettering across the top and old-fashioned candy boxes propped in the window. I walked inside.

Tony Rodriguez was there, brooding at the counter over what looked like a root beer float. He dwarfed everyone else in the place—the young woman with two preschoolers, the well-heeled Anglo couple who might have wandered over from Noe Valley, four old men rolling dice at a back table, the buxom waitresses, and me, certainly. I still couldn't get this soda shop to jive with my image of Rodriguez. But maybe that was just it. Maybe he wouldn't run into anyone he knew at a place that served open-faced tuna salad sandwiches and hot-fudge sundaes smothered with homemade marshmallows and whipped cream.

I went over and sat on a stool beside him. *"Buenos dias,"* I began.

"Talk English."

"English, yes." I started over, fighting back a wave of self-consciousness. "Mr. Rodriguez, look, I don't mean to put you on the spot here, but I need to know what Philip Gold was doing down at the site —"

"I *told* you that." Rodriguez glared at me. He had full lips, and his dark eyes were shadowed by wide brows flecked with premature gray. I noticed a similar sprinkling in the curly hairs poking out from the V of his T-shirt. He was quite a handsome fellow.

I said: "Yeah, I know, Gold worked for the city. But he was a planner, a bureaucrat. He reviewed project designs. What was he doing there *that* day? After construction had already begun?"

A waitress paused in front of us, giving Rodriguez an excuse to stall. I scanned the lime-green wall behind her. It was decorated with curving pink mosaic mirrors and super-realist paintings of pie slices, sandwiches and shakes. The choices were too overwhelming, so I simply asked for a chocolate malted. She turned around and got busy with my order. Rodriguez was still close-mouthed beside me.

"Well?" I prompted.

He scooped out a dollop of ice cream and waved the spoon angrily in front of me. "Miss, I didn't kill that guy." He dumped the cold mess into his mouth.

"Okay. So who do you think did?"

"I think he wandered onto a dark lot late at night." Rodriguez shrugged. "Somebody mugged him."

"Well, what were *you* doing there in the middle of the night?"

He tapped his spoon against the counter. "I work there. I forgot something."

Damn. This was going nowhere. Everybody worked there so nothing was fishy. I listened to Rodriguez beat a tune on the countertop and waited for my malted. It arrived in two containers, one a slender fluted glass and the other a silver cup beaded with moisture. I slurped some of the chocolate slush before picking up the thread of conversation.

"So you say you forgot something at the site. Was it the manila envelope?"

Rodriguez didn't answer. But he surprised me with a question of his own. And with his sudden vehemence. "Who are you really working for?" he demanded.

As I struggled to recall my lie, he thundered, "You're working for Budget Barn, goddammit. You can tell those sons of bitches to go to hell. I gave 'em the goddamn envelope!"

I almost fell off my stool. The Noe Valley duo looked up

with alarm from their banana split. The waitresses exchanged glances and wandered toward the back to confer. I put my hand on Rodriguez' forearm and asked, "What was in the envelope?"

He jerked back his arm. "They didn't tell you?"

I shrugged noncommitally.

He scowled, then shook his head. "Gold was calling off the deal. It was a letter with his final invoice. I turned it in, like always. That's why I went back that night, to give Gold the final payment. We always did it at night, you know, to keep it quiet. But now I'm done—I just want to do my job. Tell them that!"

I thought fast, then let out a big theatrical sigh. "Mr. Rodriguez, I think Budget Barn is jerking us both around."

He frowned.

"They didn't tell me about the deal," I went on, taking a sip of malted. "Gold's deal, I mean."

"No? So why'd they hire you? Because of the murder? To clean up the image of their precious little store?" He ended with a disdainful laugh.

I raised my brows.

Rodriguez snarled and shoved away his empty glass. "They wanna frame me, right? Those *pendejos,* they fucking did it!"

"They did?! You know that for sure?"

"No, I don't know *for sure,*" he said mockingly. "But that's what I think."

Well. I freshened my beverage with some malted from the silver cup. I could have been a chemistry nerd passing an experiment between test tubes. I slurped the drink and felt my brain clicking, trying to keep pace. Damn—I wanted to get back to the topic of Gold's "deal."

"Mr. Rodriguez," I ventured. "What was Gold's deal?"

He fixed me with his near-black eyes. "Lady, I don't know you, but I'd stay away from those people if I were you." He heaved his shoulders. "I would if I could."

"Budget Barn?"

I heard him mutter something, maybe some other expletive I'm not familiar with. Suddenly, he was Mr. Solicitous, helping out a fellow victim of the wily Budget Barn. "Yeah," he said in a low voice. "You know what they were doing? They were paying off Gold. Bribing him so they could slip through the civic review process...."

"Really?" I implored.

"Uh-huh. And they're bypassing parts of the building code, a couple of city ordinances. Saving all kinds of money."

"With Gold's help?"

"Yup."

"So...when Gold wanted out of the deal...they killed him so he wouldn't squeal?"

He shrugged. "I dunno. Maybe."

"Why did Gold call it off?"

"I dunno," he repeated, twisting his head from side to side.

Uh-oh. Rodriguez was tensing up again. I said carefully, "Did you mention this to the cops?"

"Miss," he said, his sculpted lips turning down, "I'm the middle man, remember?"

Of course. I kicked myself and tried to regain a hold on the exchange. But Rodriguez was slipping away, surly now and suspicious.

I tried jocularity. "Shit, maybe I *will* tell Budget Barn to shove it. Want to join me?"

"I don't have that option," he said coldly. "Just tell 'em to leave me alone. Let me do my job."

I looked at Rodriguez, a big, serious man, broad-shouldered and Latino. I wondered what leverage Budget Barn had over him that forced him to do their dirty work and keep on showing up to punch the clock. I had one idea.

He stood and rooted in his pocket for some bills. I got up, too. "Listen," I said, adding my own couple of dollars to the pile. "How do you know Tucker Myles?"

I'd cooled off inside the shop, but now I felt warm again as I stood next to Rodriguez, his own body heat cranked up towards a boiling point. I pressed on. "I found her phone number on a slip of paper. You know, at the site. You must have dropped it...."

Tony Rodriguez stared me down. Neither of us spoke. A mini-gang of pre-teens straggled in and started haranguing the waitresses. Instead of answering my question, my companion turned abruptly and walked out, bowling over a few unlucky squirts who blocked his path. I asked for a container to go and followed along behind him, still sucking on my cold, wet, and absurdly delicious chocolate malted.

20

I tailed Rodriguez. It was nothing flashy or sophisticated or even particularly surreptitious. I just padded along on my trusty Keds, hanging back about half a block. I wanted to see where he lived. If he had bothered to turn around, he could have seen me. But he didn't.

The foreman walked over to Potrero Avenue and turned left. I followed at a fast clip as we made time down the sidewalk across from San Francisco General Hospital. He went as far as 22nd Street, then rounded the corner. Just as I caught up, I saw him slip through a door at the top of a set of dusty red cement steps. The building was one down from the corner of Potrero, a plain-fronted stucco duplex with scarred wooden doors and metal grating over the ground floor windows.

I cooled my heels behind a clump of bushy ferns. When my watch read 5:00 p.m. I gave up the vigil. Nobody had come or gone through Rodriguez' front door. I hustled back to 24th and hunted for a phone booth. I was in luck. The first one I found had a relatively intact set of Yellow Pages hinged onto the small silver shelf.

Budget Barn was listed at an address on Bush Street. From the number, I could tell it was smack in downtown San Francisco. There was an 800 phone listing; still, I figured the local corporate offices were down on Bush. I wondered what I could find there late on a Sunday afternoon. I wondered if I should call the cops. I thought about my clients— Christa Lovett the former and Henry Gravatt the current— and their mutual antipathy for the police. Ditto Tony Rodriguez, a man I suspected of lacking a green card. I didn't want to spill his tale to the powers that be.

Damn, I was in a bind. I walked slowly back to the Mustang, head to the sidewalk, analyzing what it meant that Philip Gold had accepted bribes from Budget Barn.

For one thing, it meant he had more money then was commonly known. Unless whoever grabbed Ellen Norway knew it. I wondered, yet again, how Tucker Myles fit in, and how she knew Tony Rodriguez. Plus, how did Gold keep his skullduggery from his colleagues at the Arts Commission? Or at City Planning?

I realized another implication of this recent discovery: the union-busting, small business-squashing slime dog Budget Barn was even more corrupt than I thought. I decided to take a run down to Bush Street after all.

Traffic was pleasantly light as I cruised across town. I fiddled with the radio knob and learned that the Cubs had pulverized the Giants this afternoon at the Stick. I fiddled some more and heard some news. The Soviet Union continued to crumble. Confirmation hearings were about to begin for Supreme Court nominee Clarence Thomas. Further evidence had been uncovered implicating Bush in the ongoing Irangate saga. I sighed and kept twisting the dial. I stopped at KSAN and listened to the plaintive croon of Hank Williams. Senior, that is.

There were plenty of meters to pick from when I reached the appropriate block of Bush Street. I rolled to a stop and looked up, startled to note I'd parked right across the road from the mouth of Dashiell Hammett Street. When the gumshoe-turned-scribe lived here, it was called Monroe, but the city had renamed the street in his honor. I smiled and peered up the block to my right. Yup, Burritt Street. I locked the car and strolled to the alley, playing literary tourist. A copper plaque was fastened to the gray cement wall at the opening of Burritt. It read: "On approximately this spot, Miles Archer, partner of Sam Spade, was done in by Brigid O'Shaughnessy."

I rotated, imagining the fog-shrouded scene in the dead of night when Spade pulled up in a Yellow Cab to find his partner spread-eagled on a slab of rock halfway down a dirt slope. Now, the lot was occupied by a Chinese restaurant and a food market with grime-coated windows. I walked past the Tunnel Top Bar and stood at the hatched iron railing. Beneath me, cars flowed through the Stockton Tunnel en route to Chinatown, trailing a steady stream of exhaust that wafted up the stairwells on either side of the passageway. I imagined the steps looked much like they did in Hammett's time: ugly, barren, the walls limned with decades of dirt and residue. Only now, the flickering neon lights of the Green Door massage parlor greeted pedestrians who ventured down one set of dingy stairs.

I turned to scope out the far side of Bush. The buildings there had undergone an upgrade. A spiffy hotel sat on one corner, a buff-fronted office building on the other. The number confirmed it: Budget Barn was in the corner building. I trotted across, dodging the sparse flow of one-way traffic. The glass doors fronting the street were unlocked so I stepped through into a hushed corridor lined with gilt-edged mirrors. A pair of elevators sat at the end of the hall, topped by old-fashioned floor indicators with little brass arrows. As I got closer, I saw a discreet directory sandwiched between the doors—it told me Budget Barn was four floors up.

In the minutes I spent riding the elevator and skulking around the fourth floor, I didn't see a soul. The Budget Barn offices were locked tight behind a set of black double doors. A rectangular pane of glass rested alongside, but it was the kind of smoked, beveled glass meant for decoration, not visibility. Two more doors further down the hallway may have been exits for Budget Barn. One was locked. The other, to my surprise, fell open when I turned the knob.

I flipped a light and found myself inside a utility closet, a coffin-sized space jammed with cleaning supplies. Shelves ran all the way up to the ceiling on one side. This seemed to be a dumping zone for overflow office supplies, too; I spied cartons of $8^1/_2$" x 11" paper and a stash of envelopes printed with a Budget Barn logo. I snickered, eyeing the little redwood barn with a dollar sign for a weathervane.

I returned to the corridor and shut the closet behind me, then cast another glance up and down the hall. I decided to eschew my usual approach: break-in first, ask questions later. Instead, I'd come back Monday and see what kind of bargain I could finagle with the corporate wizards of the cut-rate deal.

I detoured by Tennessee Street on the way to my dinner date. I had a little time to kill. I wanted to brush my teeth, collect my wits, put some business in order.

Mary appeared to have tornadoed through the warehouse in a cleaning frenzy. The place was tidy. And instead of the usual odors, I smelled ammonia, lemon cleanser, and the fresh perfume of freesias. Mary had left the flowers on my desk in a makeshift vase fashioned from a paint can. A note was pinned underneath. She told me she was beginning her move to Emeryville—and reminded me I better get scrambling.

Yeah. Shoot. I balled the note and tossed it in the trash. Then I went to freshen up in the bathroom.

When I got back to the desk, I hit the phone machine and listened to the scratchy whir of rewinding tape. Only two messages since yesterday: Margaret Halliway, Luchetti's lover and San Francisco's DA, wanted to talk to me about Lydia. And Ms. John Lennon called from the Cathedral Hill Hotel to whisper that Christa Lovett had vanished. She hadn't formally checked out, but all her significant personal items were gone and the hotel staff hadn't seen her in days. They figured she'd split town in a hurry. *À bientôt. Ciao. Hasta luego.*

I plunked into my leather chair and stretched my arms over my head. Damn it all. Suddenly, the last thing I wanted to do was chitchat with a new acquaintance over a sure-to-be candlelit dinner. Instead, I felt like sharing Hot 'N Hunky burgers with Phoebe, maybe hearing about her Saturn return woes or her day at the races.

I sighed and turned my thoughts back to Lovett. Either she left town in frustration or something had happened to her. I went back to my desk and fished out the notebook with the info I'd pilfered from Lovett's passport. AT&T gave me a phone number that purportedly matched her Lyndale Avenue address in Minneapolis. When I called, the ringing went on and on—no answer, no machine, no sad-voiced woman with a secret came on the line to quell all my worries.

Well, I figured, I'd already washed my hands of Christa Lovett. As if to prove it to myself, I pulled her client file and straightened out the minimal paperwork. Then I typed a final report using an outmoded sheet of carbon paper, and stuck one copy of the report in an envelope for Lovett. I wrote out her Lyndale Avenue address and plastered a stamp on the corner. If I had an "out" box, that's where it would have gone.

Next I busily constructed a clean file folder for Henry Gravatt. I filled it with a page full of scrawled notes, a new contract, and—on further thought—most of the contents of Lovett's file. I put a copy of the contract in an envelope for Gravatt and stamped it, too. I'd post both mailings on my way out. Then I stuck the rest of the mess in the file cabinet under "G."

Whew. I savored my organizational accomplishment for a while, munching a few of the Fig Newtons I'd left stranded in the drawer. Then I picked up the phone to call Meg Halliway. I couldn't reach her at home so I left an awkward message of sympathy on her answering machine and called the hospital. Halliway had left. Shoot. But another nurse repeated what I'd heard that morning: Lydia's condition was stable but critical. She still hadn't spoken.

Finally, I checked my next destination on a San Francisco map. Princess lived on Newhall Street in the Bayview district, not far from the Hunter's Point shipyards. I didn't get down there that often. I memorized a route and retired the map. Then I squared my shoulders and headed out the door. Shouldn't keep the princess waiting.

21

As it turned out, Princess Bafaloukos wasn't the candle-light type. She wasn't much for chitchat either, at least not when she had grander designs in mind. She fed me pirosh-kis, beet salad, and cole slaw from a take-out joint on outer Geary—"You'll love it, Nell," she purred, "it's called the Tip Toe Inn"—then squired me upstairs to the roof.

The night air was cold, and I swore I saw a star or two hanging low in the sky over the distant hills of Oakland. Princess had an elaborate lounge setup on the rooftop, com-plete with a heating lamp like the kind restaurants use on their outdoor patios. A raised platform featured a queen-sized futon piled high with blankets. Music was piped in through a pair of compact speakers, and a cooler kept a bottle of champagne iced up. I felt like I'd stumbled into a Seven-ties bachelor pad—er, make that a bachlorette pad.

I don't much care for champagne, but when Princess popped the cork and sidled over with a glassful, I accepted gratefully. I figured it couldn't hurt.

"Look," I said, and twisted away to walk across the tar. I stopped at the edge and gestured into the void.

Princess stepped into place alongside me. "What do you see?" she asked, resting an arm ever so lightly across my shoulders.

I was surprised to feel a tremor run down my spine and settle somewhere south of the border. I caught my breath and said, "In the water. The lights."

A tanker was gliding smoothly around the tip of Hunter's Point, its illuminated deck twinkling with the eerie glow of a ghost ship. I turned slowly to take in the whole vista. Princess lived on the top floor of a house at the crest of Newhall and Quesada Avenue. The rooftop, secluded enough to ensure privacy, was also so high that a panoramic view opened up on three sides: Candlestick Park to the south, the produce district to the north, and the old shipyards to the east. This was a solidly working-class neighborhood, but from on high, the region gave off the sparkling illusion of a magic kingdom.

Suddenly I laughed.

"What?" Princess probed me with her eyes.

"Check out the edge of the building." I pointed to the row of protruding stucco rectangles and the fortified buttresses in the corners. "Your house is shaped like a medieval castle."

Her hair gel glistened in the dark. "Sweetheart, that's why I moved here," she teased, then bent down and brushed her lips against mine.

I reached up to put a hand behind her neck. It felt sinewy and taut. I ran my palm across her collarbone and down her back. Princess wore another denim shirt, this one washed so

146

many times it seemed like a second layer of skin. It was wild. She was soft and hard all at once, a pillar of strength with a velvety veneer and a set of lips that knew their business. I drew closer. Her hands were up inside my sweater doing something marvelous at the small of my back. Before I could say "latex," we had pirouetted back across the tar and into the warm zone of the heating lamp. Through the speakers, I could hear Harry Connick, Jr. trying to be Sinatra, and here I was, trying to be Susie Bright.

"Hang on," I squeaked. I sat on the edge of the bed and tried to get my bearings. Bubbles tickled my throat when I poured in champagne. Above me, Princess was situated against the night sky like some kind of buff goddess. I smiled shyly and said, "Will you respect me in the morning?"

Princess cracked up and belly-flopped onto the bed. "Nell," she guffawed, "you are a piece of work."

She had deposited her champagne someplace so she took a sip of mine. Then she rooted around under the futon frame and drew out a cylindrical tin that used to hold butter cookies. She flipped the lid to reveal a pastel assortment of gloves, condoms, and rectangular swatches. A few leather accessories appeared to be buried down below. I picked up a latex square and said, "You think these are necessary?"

Princess shrugged. "Don't know about that. But they can be fun." She reached for my hand and began drawing a fingertip into her mouth. Then she turned the hand gently and asked, "What did you do to your palm?"

"Oh. I...scraped 'em."

Princess smiled triumphantly and tossed me a pair of turquoise latex gloves. "See? That's why these things come in handy."

I dutifully snapped on the gloves and pretended to play doctor for a while, giving Princess a thorough examination. Then I pressed against her side and got serious. I told her about having herpes. She told me about past forays with a different gender. We were being so responsible I suggested we volunteer for a safer sex TV ad. Princess poked me in the ribs and threatened to go get her video camera.

"Kinky!" I laughed, and rolled over to pin her to the mattress.

But Princess was stronger than I was and had me on my back in a flash. The wrestling felt good, hearty, just what I needed to make my mind unbend for a while. At one point, I looked at her face and felt a shock of strangeness—who was this woman with the cleft chin, smooth brow, and glint of acquisitiveness in her eyes? But when I slipped my hand between her legs and felt her sopping warmth and a rush of breath along my neck, everything seemed okay again. I kissed her hard and whispered something meaningless in her ear.

Princess was one of these multi-orgasmic types who could probably come in five seconds with the aid of a feather duster. I helped her along, enjoying the novelty of the open air and the unfamiliar rhythms of a near stranger. I didn't come, myself. That was fine. By the time we gathered our scattered clothing and headed downstairs I was pretty tuckered out, but contented nonetheless. I'd had two affairs since meeting Rae, and each time I'd felt wise and worldly, one more dyke keeping the world safe for nonmonogamy. Here I was, doing it again.

"Thanks for the dinner, Princess." She really was something, I thought, watching her plop Sade into the CD player. She'd put her shirt on, but the backs of her thighs were visible below the hem, lean and cut like an athlete's.

She swiveled her head and said, "Can't you stick around?"

I smiled and told her about Pinky. Princess brought out two glasses of water and we lingered for a bit. She had the usual questions about private eyeing, which I mostly deflected. When I asked about her job, she shrugged and said that working for the station was good experience, but she really wanted to develop her own projects.

"Like what?"

"Documentaries, mostly. I'm kind of a history buff." She slicked back her hair and looked almost shy. "I'm interested in women's labor history. But right now I'm helping a friend make a video about women at Lexington. You know, the prison."

"Oh yeah?" Princess Bafaloukos could surprise me yet.

"Yeah, the conditions are still horrible, even after they shut down the High Security Unit. Some of the political prisoners have been locked up for years without even getting a trial...."

I'd read about the federal pen in Lexington, Kentucky, and its infamous sensory deprivation unit. I remembered, too, that some of the more vocal women had been transferred to other prisons around the country—the old divide-and-conquer strategy.

Princess explained the focus of her friend's video. "It's about women who were revolutionaries on the *outside* who continue to agitate on the *inside*. Like, by organizing AIDS education programs or anti-racism workshops. Or by protesting the brutality of the guards." She shook her head. "One of the women we interviewed was underground for almost ten years before she got caught."

"Ten years? Wow." I chugged some water.

"Yeah—can you imagine? She was involved in that famous Brinks robbery. But you know, ten years is nothing. Some of those radicals—like from the Sixties—they're still fugitives."

I stared at Bafaloukos.

"What, you don't believe me? I've been doing lots of research—"

"No, I believe you." I stopped. "Princess...."

"What? What's wrong?"

I stood and took a stroll around her living room. I stopped in front of a blond wood bookcase and asked, "Do you have any research materials handy? Like articles and books and stuff?"

"Some." She was eyeing me quizzically.

"Sorry," I laughed. "I just got this crazy idea."

"I'll say."

"Do you think I could borrow some of your reading materials? I'd like to bone up on it."

"Well..." She walked over and scanned the bookshelves. "*I* know."

She left the room and returned in a moment with a bulging brown accordion file. "Here. This is a project description and budget for the video. And some of the articles I used for background. I won't need these for a while. I'm mostly editing interview footage right now."

"Thanks." I leaned up and kissed her cheek.

She took advantage of the moment and crushed me close in her arms. "I guess this means you'll be back?" she whispered.

"Unless I decide to go underground...."

As I piloted the Mustang north over surface streets, I

thought how wild it would be to disappear, to simply drop out of sight. I pondered the circumstances that might drive a person underground, away from the oppressive grip of the law. I thought of famous one-time fugitives like Susan Saxe, Fred Hampton, Kathy Boudin and Leonard Peltier. I considered Patty Hearst. Which lead, of course, to crazy thoughts about a trio of contemporary women who were suddenly nowhere to be found—the kidnapped Norway, the creepy Myles, and the lovely, elusive Christa Lovett.

I was so preoccupied, in fact, that I failed to see the man in the steel gray Mercury who fell into traffic behind me and parked at the far end of Ramona, watching with cold, yellow eyes as I unlocked my apartment door and stepped inside.

22

Pinky had fallen asleep with the light on, *Goat Song* spread-eagled on the covers. I tiptoed over to snap off her lamp. Then I propped myself up in bed with the contents of the accordion file scattered all around me.

I read all of it: articles about prisoners and HIV, recountings of the Brinks robbery and the D.C. Resistance Conspiracy Case, first-person stories from a number of former fugitives and current inmates. So much idealism, so much strife—all in the name of peace and freedom.

I was especially interested in Kathy Boudin, a founder of the original Weather Underground, and Susan Saxe, a woman involved in the theft of classified—and highly damaging—U.S. Army documents. She was also a participant in the famous 1970 Boston bank heist during which a cop was killed. Saxe came out as a lesbian while underground, and her case stirred great dissension among feminists. Some wanted to embrace her, others to distance her from the movement.

Other women fueled similar ruptures among Second Wavers, or continued to do so today. Some of the names rung a bell, but many were new to me—Norma Jean Croy, Jane Alpert, Amanda McCracken, Silvia Baraldini, Marylou Blackwomon. By the time I finished reading, my mind was buzzing with possibilities.

I finished *In the Game* before falling asleep. It was a crack-up. Then I picked up Susan Faludi's *Backlash* and rested the weighty tome in my hands. Time to start the ballyhooed new feminist classic. But I just wasn't in the mood. I sighed and reached for the light.

This time, my dreams were free of Cher and friends. Instead, a coterie of bomb-toting gals of all colors kept me company through the night, Christa Lovett among them. She wore a tight black turtleneck, bell-bottomed jeans, and a swingin' peace symbol pendant around her neck like a sacred badge of honor.

I was up before Pinky, not fully rested but ready to roll nonetheless. The first thing I did, post-coffee, was dial up District Attorney Margaret Halliway. Finally, she was home—she answered on the first ring.

I said: "Meg. Hi, it's Nell Fury."

"Nell." Halliway sighed.

"I'm...sorry." Boy. What an understatement.

Meg seemed to understand that words were inadequate. I asked about Lydia. Apparently she was holding steady, but there'd been no improvement. Meg said she was on her way back to the hospital now, then heading into the office.

When I asked how she was doing, Meg said, "Okay," but I could tell she was in her brisk professional mode. She'd never shared feelings with me before, and I didn't expect her to start now. Instead, she asked about the night I found Lydia. I gave her my version of the story. She grunted when I finished.

"Meg, what's the latest theory?"

"They think it was Tucker Myles."

"Based on what evidence?"

"All I know is that Myles registered a 9mm Beretta some time ago—it's a possible match with the bullet and cartridge casing. Plus, she's disappeared. If the police have anything more solid, they're not telling me."

"What about the Oakland DA?"

"They won't discuss it." Halliway was pissed.

"Meg," I said slowly, "do you know why Lydia was there that night? Outside Myles' apartment? Did you find any of her notes or anything?"

"Noooo…" She paused conspicuously. Hmm. Before I could press further, she asked, "Why were *you* there, Nell?"

"Oh." Shit. "I was on a case. To do with the Philip Gold murder. You know, Tucker Myles works with Gold's fiancée—"

"Yeah, I know. What else do you know about her?"

"Who? Ellen Nor—"

"*Myles.*"

I was beginning to remember why I didn't like Halliway. But Lydia Luchetti was my friend, too. I hung in there. "Myles and Ellen Norway are lovers. I'm trying to find them both. If Myles really did it, I'll help bring her in. I promise." Geez, I sounded like some hard-nosed vigilante.

Halliway whistled. "Ellen Norway? And Myles? Jesus."

"What's the word on the kidnapping?"

"No more phone calls. The police think it was a setup."

"You mean, like staged—"

"Yeah, I wonder—" Margaret clicked her teeth. "I wonder if Lydia figured it out. She figured that Norway staged her own kidnapping, with Myles help. And maybe Lydia found them. But why would...huh."

Halliway was sharp, I'll give her that. But I knew one other thing she didn't know. Philip Gold had been wealthier then he seemed. If Norway and Myles were aware of that, they would have known they could bilk him for a hefty sum. But why bother, if Ellen was planning to marry him anyway? I chuckled. Of course—then she wouldn't *have* to marry him. Norway and Myles could have each other *and* the extra dough.

So did they kill Gold and go after Luchetti, too? What about Budget Barn? Something seemed off....

Halliway was asking me a question. I tuned back in. "Huh?"

"Nell, did you hear me? I said, keep it under wraps, about Norway's kidnapping—"

"Right."

"—because of the child, Rosie, and the parents. The police are playing it cool. They don't want to alarm them until they know something definite."

"Gotcha."

I felt lousy after we rang off. I wanted to think of the three missing women as rebels with a cause; instead, they seemed more and more like plain old thugs, motivated by greed. I still couldn't figure Lovett, though. But wherever

156

she was, I suspected Norway and Myles were hovering somewhere in the wings.

Suddenly, I felt like I was running in place on a treadmill. I sketched some notes and tried to prioritize things. My immediate goals were threefold: find Norway and Myles, expose the Budget Barn shenanigans, and discover who went after Luchetti. Or, more simply, find the common ground among all three and watch the pieces fall into place. I hurriedly formulated a plan and got back on the phone.

First, I placed a check-in call to Henry Gravatt. He wasn't at work yet, so I left a message with the nasal-voiced temp. Then I phoned the staff accountant at the San Francisco Arts Commission and got the big-time brush-off. He said he had no comment—Commissioner Stan Raphaelson was handling all calls. I told him I wasn't with the press, but the fact didn't penetrate. He just babbled Raphaelson's number and hustled off the line.

Damn. The Arts Commission was running scared. Was the public pressure getting to them or did they really have something to hide? I wondered if anyone else knew about Gold's alleged bribe-taking. Hmm. I remembered Stan Raphaelson was Gold's co-chair on the civic design review committee. I punched in seven digits, and heard the drone of an answering machine. I asked Raphaelson to call me, ASAP, and left both my numbers.

I tried calling Rosie Norway, too, but struck out once more. Mrs. Zimmer answered. Though perfectly civil, she ran interference with a clearly fabricated excuse about errands, cramps, a headache, and a shower. All at once, eh? But she told me Rosie was fine, so I guess I had to leave it at that. Mrs. Zimmer signed off with a nervous twitter to her salutation.

I was foraging hopelessly through my barren cupboards when Pinky detoured into the kitchenette. Her hair was plastered down on one side, her eyes ringed with yesterday's smudged eyeliner. A lump rose up in my throat so I didn't say anything right away.

"Hey," she mumbled.

I walked over to give her a tousle.

"Where were you last night, Mum? Rae came by."

"She did?!"

Pinky poured some dark French roast. "You didn't tell me she was moving. That's so intense—"

"I thought she had plans for last night!"

Pinky gave me a weird look. "She said she got out of 'em—she wanted to see you." Pinky blew into her cup. "What's the big deal?"

"Ahh...nothing." Damn.

Pinky walked away chuckling.

I got dressed. Gray trousers, white button-down shirt, and molded old oxfords. When Pinky reappeared in a black jumper and flawless makeup job, I asked her to join me for breakfast. Over buckwheat cakes and syrup at the It's Tops· Coffee Shop, we discussed the loose ends of the Lovett case, Pinky's latest batch of poems, and my fantasy plans for a trip to London. I think we talked about the weather, too, before moving on to Tammie Rae's departure. Pinky was awfully mature about it, advising me to hang tough and persuade Rae to move back in a year.

I was mopping up the last bit of syrup when someone at a booth got busy with the tabletop jukebox. Janis moaned, "...one day up near Salinas, Lord, I let him slip away..."

I dropped a couple of five-spots and followed Pinky out the door.

23

The Mustang needed a tank of gas and a scrubdown. The latter could wait, but I cruised over to a self-serve on South Van Ness and juiced her up. I'd arranged to meet Pinky and Rae for dinner. I wondered how much I could accomplish between now and then.

First stop: Budget Barn. It wasn't too wise to drive downtown on a busy Monday morning, but I was feeling a bit reckless. I even put the top down and stuck my arm out the side, carving miniature waves in the air with my hand. When I got to Bush and Burritt, all the mystique of the day before had evaporated. The neighborhood hummed with commerce, a hectic workaday feel more tedious than evocative of times past. I drove around the block and dumped the car in the Sutter-Stockton garage. Then I traipsed past the Green Door massage parlor, up the Stockton Tunnel stairwell, and into the spiffy office building on the opposite corner.

This time, people were in and out, up and down the elevators, crawling all over the joint. I hadn't planned on being sneaky, but as I passed through the hall of mirrors I spied a familiar set of shoulders entering one of the elevators. I hugged the wall and sprinted, just in time to verify that foreman Tony Rodriguez was indeed getting swallowed up by the sliding doors. Wow. I was pretty sure he didn't see me. I quickly scanned the corridor and found the stairs off to one side. I took them two at a time and emerged, puffing, onto the fourth floor.

I edged slowly toward the Budget Barn doors. Then I gasped as I heard the elevator stop with a thud behind me. Damn, I'd actually beaten Rodriguez. Chatter from the opening doors began leaking into the corridor. I darted down the hall, hoping to keep out of sight. Aha! The utility closet. I tugged—it was still unlocked and unoccupied. I slipped inside, feeling my heart kick up a commotion on the inside of my chest. I pressed my back against the inner wall, trying to calm down and strategize.

That's when I discovered the closet was adjacent to somebody's office. The acoustics were distorted but clear enough to pick up voices. I put one ear right up to a crack in the cheap plywood siding and heard a man say, "He's here? Umm. Uh-huh. Shit. I don't care—if he won't do it, he's history, got that?"

The fellow paused. Then he resumed, "Ohhhhh-kay. Send him in."

I concentrated. I heard a door click open and shut. There was some rustling and scraping, then Tony Rodriguez said, "Leonard, I'm through with this."

"*Señor*." Leonard's voice was layered with treacle and condescension. "Have a seat. Let's not be hasty."

160

Apparently, Rodriguez kept standing, because I heard the sound of heavy footsteps and what might have been a boot slamming into a piece of furniture. He said testily, "Screw it. I want Gold's file. I want you to get rid of any records on me—"

Leonard butted in. "Hey, chill out, man. There's no mention—"

"Like hell! I know what you're doing. You're trying to pin—"

"*Tony.*" There went the sarcasm. "We have enough leverage over you without leaving a paper trail. Really."

"Jesus, Leonard. I cooperated with the cops. I kept you out of it. And I do my fucking job. Isn't that enough?"

Leonard laughed. "What's the matter? You want a vacation? Fine—a trip for two to sunny San Salvador. Let me just get on the horn to the INS travel agency..." He ended with a snort.

Silence.

I listened to someone's foot prattle in the hallway and the rhythmic pound of my heartbeat. I kept waiting. A phone jangled in another office. Finally Leonard said, "Tony, man, we appreciate you. We really do. And the good news is, we found another inside contact. If *you* don't want to deal, we can always get someone else to take your job. There's plenty..."

Damn! A fax machine hummed into action in one of the surrounding offices. Mr. Sarcasm's words got lost in the rattle. When the noise died down, I picked up the gist of it.

"...will take Gold's place," Leonard was saying. "So. Can we count on you, Senor Rodriguez?"

Huh. Either Tony agreed to continue as the middle man for Budget Barn's secret deals with the city, or he got deported. I'd missed the name of Gold's replacement. Shoot. I wondered if the company really did keep a file on their dirty deeds. I was wondering how to get inside Leonard's inner sanctum when I heard Tony say, "All right. But remember, I kept the cops out of your hair. So you call off the lady."

"The lady?"

"The private eye."

Uh-oh.

"What are you talking about?" Leonard asked.

"The fucking spy. What's her name, Nell…"

The fax machine purred. Damn technology! I fidgeted, waiting for the noise to subside. When I could hear again, I caught Leonard in an outright lie. "…oh yeah, Nell Fury. Right. Sure, man…"

Oh boy. If I wasn't in deep shit before, I was now.

"…we'll take care of it," he finished.

Rodriguez spoke. "Just call her off, that's all. She asked about Tucker Myles, but I don't think she knows they've gone to Minneapolis."

I jumped. *Minneapolis.*

"Hmm." Leonard spoke softly. "Tony?"

"What?"

"How do *you* know about that?" His voice was deadly sober now.

"Well…fuck, I talked to Tucker. Big deal. She was following Gold around, or something, I don't know. She saw us together once and gave me her phone number. So what?"

"Hmm." I heard something slam, maybe a book on a table. Maybe a palm. "You shouldn't be messing with Tucker. That's my *private* thing. Nobody else knows about Minneapolis."

"Well, forget it. I'm not gonna say anything…Jesus,

what are you doing…?"

Suddenly, a loud crack exploded from inside, and the sounds of a scuffle echoed through the thin wall. It got louder. Footsteps started pounding from more than one direction. I hugged the wall and squeezed my eyes shut.

Tony Rodriguez shouted, "Gimme that!" Then I heard a sickening crunch followed by a loud thump. More footsteps. "Stop him!" somebody yelled. I poked my head out the closet door just in time to see Rodriguez barrel out the doors of Budget Barn corporate headquarters, a large black notebook secured under one arm. He flew to the stairwell.

I didn't think it through. I just sprinted along behind him, abandoning the commotion in the office suite. I heard another figure run after us, but whoever it was yelled "Fuck!" and gave up the chase at the top of the stairs. Maybe nobody besides Leonard knew the significance of the notebook in Tony's clutches.

Rodriguez tripped helter-skelter down four flights and out the front doors to Bush Street. I couldn't tell if he knew I was there, too, hurdling along like a contender in some wacky obstacle race. Rodriguez dove across traffic and down the steps that hugged the Stockton Tunnel. I wasn't nearly as swift crossing Bush Street. But I took the stairs at breakneck speed, dodging a handful of habitués who were having a much more leisurely Monday than I.

As I rounded the bend, I saw Rodriguez leap off the curb, apparently heading across the road for the Sutter-Stockton garage. At the same instant, I saw the nose of a gleaming white limo zoom from the mouth of the Stockton Tunnel. I watched—as if caught in slow motion—as the front bumper plowed into Rodriguez, flipped him into a triple spin, and sent him falling into the path of an oncoming tour bus. After that, I sank to the pavement, arm clutching my stomach. I rocked on my heels and listened as the immediate world spun into crisis mode. Car brakes and voices screeched in unison while I wept silent tears for a guy I hardly knew, much less cared for—but a person, nonetheless, who deserved something better from this crummy, heartless universe.

A horde of onlookers swarmed to the scene. I rose woozily to my feet. Right in front of me, the flickering neon of the Green Door massage parlor beckoned with lurid promise. Below the sign, a black three-ringed notebook lay split open on the sidewalk, the cover battered but the contents still intact. Jesus.

I picked up the notebook and kept walking. There was nothing I could do for Tony Rodriguez. Except, perhaps, clear his name from any damning evidence in the pages of the loose-leaf notebook.

Nobody paid me any mind. I made a beeline for the nearest public toilet I knew of, the fourth-floor restroom at Macy's Union Square. There, wedged in a stall between glazed-eyed shoppers, I vomited my breakfast and what felt like an entire week's worth of meals. Then I perched on the toilet and read the black notebook from cover to cover.

24

I stopped at the Speedy Gonzalez copy shop on Mission Street on my way to the office. I dropped a bundle making five copies of the Budget Barn secret dossier, excising all mention of Tony Rodriguez.

When I got to the warehouse, I carefully collated the pile and assembled five identical envelopes. I addressed one to each of the dailies, one to City Supervisor Jed Flack, and one to the SFPD, attention Fraud Section of the Bureau of Inspectors. I wasn't sure that was the right division, but I figured it was a place to start. All the envelopes were anonymous except for the fifth—that one went to Tad Greenblatt with a note to sequester it immediately in the Continent West vault.

I locked the original notebook in my own mini-safe. Then I devoured the veggie burrito I'd picked up at El Toro.

The notebook confirmed what Tony Rodriguez had told me. In order to bypass costly environmental regulations, a couple of city ordinances, and the Arts Commission design review process, Budget Barn had been bribing Philip Gold. Apparently, he'd been able to facilitate the scam by falsifying records both at the Commission and at City Planning. The notebook included an accounting of the dates and amounts of the transactions, which roughly involved a payoff of about $2,000 every other week. It had been going on for over three years.

Other papers summarized conversations Budget Barn executives had had with Gold and Rodriguez. Also included were reports on meetings with small business owners in the South of Market area, and notes on union-thwarting strategies. Hmm. The spiral notebook seemed to be Leonard's own little profit-maximizing manual. Neither he nor any other Budget Barn exec was named. Still, I figured between the newspapers, City Hall, and the boys in blue, somebody would find a way to nail the scumbags.

One other item of note: a page of information about Tucker Myles. It mentioned a bit about her background, her relation to Gold, and her potential as a collaborator. It also appeared she'd been receiving payoffs. Whew—a double scam artist. My best guess was that Myles found out about Gold's deal and demanded hush money from Budget Barn. I'd never know for sure if I didn't find her. Unless someone else found her. She was, after all, still the number one suspect in the attack on Luchetti.

I knew Myles had gone to Minneapolis, Christa Lovett's town. Was Ellen Norway there, too? I glanced at my watch. It was only 11:30 a.m. I started formulating a crazy plan. Then I guffawed, pulled myself out of a slouch, and spun around to check my phone messages.

What I heard only fueled my wild idea.

The first caller was a frantic Mrs. Zimmer. Rosie Norway had disappeared; she'd gone to the grocery store this morning and never returned.

The second caller put the nail in the coffin. Rochelle Lamb called to say she'd be sending a list of little Roses born in the Chicago area between 1972 and 1974. But, following a tip from a helpful clerk, Lamb had crossed the border into Indiana and found the birth certificate of someone she thought was *the* Rosie Norway. Rose Ellen McCracken, born in Gary, Indiana on March 2, 1974, to Amy Norway and David McCracken.

Lamb had gone the extra mile and called the doctor listed on the birth certificate. Of course, he didn't recall the delivery. But Lamb must have sweet-talked him, because he volunteered to go back and check hospital records. What he found was an odd file that jolted his memory of the birth.

The mother had not been a regular patient. She'd come in early on a wintry morning with a woman friend, explaining that the father was away in Vietnam. The women gave a Chicago address. They left the hospital soon after delivery, despite a recommendation that the mother and child stay overnight. Then they'd never paid the bill. Hospital collectors were unable to track the women; the pursuit fizzled out and was eventually abandoned after a report was filed with authorites.

Wow. She'd left all that on my answering machine. I might have to visit the Windy City and take a lesson in thoroughness from Rochelle Lamb. Maybe Warshawski would coach me, too. Then we could all go out and get debauched together at a Cubs game. Yee haw.

Meanwhile, the name McCracken was stuck in my craw. I whipped out a notepad and wrote out David McCracken and Amy Norway. Then Rose Ellen McCracken. Why would Ellen Norway list a different first name for herself? And give her kid the real moniker as a middle name? Mc-Cracken...McCracken.

I stood and scuffed my oxfords across the expanse of cement floor. I stopped and gazed at Mary's canvas of blue and gray circles. Then it came to me. I'd read about a McCracken in the materials I'd borrowed from Princess. What was the name? Amanda. Amanda McCracken. I couldn't recall for sure, but I thought she might be one of the people responsible for a munitions plant bombing in New Jersey. Was she a former fugitive, a current fugitive, a prisoner, or none of the above?

Big deal, Fury. How many McCrackens are there in the universe? McTons. Still, I trotted back to the desk and studied the names on my notepad. Amy Norway. David Mc-Cracken. *Amy McCracken.* Damn.

I raced home to re-read the relevant part of the file. Amanda McCracken was who I thought she was—one of five people convicted in the 1971 bombing that had partially destroyed a weapons manufacturing plant. A cop had died during their failed getaway, and though Amanda wasn't the triggerwoman, she'd taken the fall along with the rest of them. After the trial, Amanda and one of the other women escaped while en route to the slammer. The other woman was shot down soon thereafter by a posse of modern-day bounty hunters. But Amanda McCracken was still at large, rumored to be a dogged, respected veteran of the underground.

I tried to picture McCracken repackaged as solid, upstanding accountant Ellen Norway. I couldn't quite see it. But I could imagine this: Ellen's new lover Tucker Myles begins to meddle in unsavory business, so Ellen starts worrying that things are getting too hot. She figures she'd better drop out of sight again. She fakes her own kidnapping, milking Gold for as much as she can. And she takes Tucker with her? And Rosie?

When Pinky walked in, she found me throwing a toothbrush and T-shirt into a canvas bag. I sat her down and gave her the old Nell Fury hard sell. Her kohl-rimmed eyes widened in astonishment, but eventually a corner of her mouth started twitching. Pinky said, "Very well then, Mum," and darted off to start packing. I guess her farewell date with Eleven that day had gone smoothly—at any rate, she was a willing accomplice to my impulsiveness.

I got busy on the phone. I called my gay travel agency— Queen City Travel—and rerouted Pinky's airline ticket. I reserved a flight of my own. Then I called Rae and moved our date forward to Tuesday night. She wasn't too happy about it, but then, neither was I. I called my big sister Grace and asked if my wayward daughter and I could crash with her that night. I even phoned Henry Gravatt and gave him a sketchy account of my current strategy. He seemed puzzled, but I didn't elaborate. Finally, I called Barbary Coast Cab and requested the services of ace driver Phoebe Grahame. The dispatcher said A-OK.

After that, I wandered over to the fish bowl to see how my little charges were doing. Flannery and Carson were performing a lazy dance, twisting in seamless tandem among the fuschia leaves of their beloved plastic plant. I sprinkled in supper and watched them scramble to the surface. Then I turned on the radio and waded through the stations until I found some news.

Among other things, I heard that a Budget Barn vice-president, Leonard Galle, was in stable condition after suffering an assault in his office. The perpetrator, Tony Rodriguez, had been struck by a bus and killed as he fled the premises. From his hospital bed, Galle said he had no idea what had enraged Rodriguez, who he described as a laborer down at the 10th and Harrison site. Galle expressed sadness over Rodriguez' death, but said he was glad the trouble was over.

It's only just begun, bucko, I muttered. Then I went to help Pinky get ready.

Ninety minutes later, we were sitting in the back of Phoebe's cab on the way to the San Francisco airport. Johnnie Blue was in the front seat. She'd been on a ride-along with Phoebe, just for fun, and decided to keep us all company. First off, I told her I was sorry to miss her comedy show the other night.

"No problem, Nell. You'll have plenty of chances. But you should catch Les & Jan sometime—they were *awesome*." Johnnie swiveled her neck and dazzled me with a smile. Her eyes were huge wet pools, her hair an angelic halo of stubby dreads. I knew what Phoebe saw in Johnnie Blue—I'd made a play for her myself.

But Phoebe, the fetching waif, had beat me out. She'd been happy-in-love ever since. So happy, in fact, that it got on my nerves sometimes. I tossed my curls and told myself to stop being a jerk about it. I was just jealous, anyway.

Phoebe was white and Johnnie African-American, and it was their one point of stress as they struggled to negotiate the vast terrain of differences. Things seemed to be going well lately. When Phoebe wasn't working, she was almost always with Johnnie. And now, it seemed, they were together during work, too. I gazed out the window and felt a pang for Rae. We'd always kept more distance than that. But 2,000 miles was a little more than I'd bargained for.

I sighed. Then said to Johnnie: "Are you working on any new material?"

"Uh-huh." She bobbed her head. "I've got this sketch going about Neil Bush—you know, presidential offspring ripping off the taxpayers. And god, I've *gotta* do something about Joe's elbow."

Everybody laughed except Pinky. "What's Joe's elbow?" she asked.

"Oh, honey," I replied, "it's…it's an American thing.…"

Pinky requested tunes. Johnnie found some devastating thrasher rock, and we rolled for a while down 101 just listening to the sounds. When we passed the Cow Palace turnoff, Phoebe lowered the volume and asked me about Lydia Luchetti. We hadn't yet discussed her condition.

I relayed the traumatic story, watching Phoebe nod her head intently. Her voice was a bit gravelly when she asked about our sudden departure.

"Phoebes," I said, "I think I know where to find the woman who did it."

Nobody posed the obvious question: why not call the cops? But I'd thought it out for myself. If I found Tucker Myles, I'd certainly bring in the big guns. But if my hunches were wrong for any reason, I didn't want to blow Amanda McCracken's cover.

Pinky piled out first when we got to the airport. I stepped to the curb clutching a spare piece of Pinky's luggage, a sunny yellow hatbox covered with black and white skull-and-crossbones. Johnnie Blue gave us each a smack. Phoebe squeezed Pinky really hard, then turned to me.

"I brought you something to read." She handed me a paperback. *Shockproof Sydney Skate*, by Marijane Meaker.

I raised a brow.

"It's hilarious," she said. "It's about a lesbian mom with a teenage kid. Kind of a Holden Caulfield type. You'll love it."

I smiled and rested a palm on Phoebe's shoulder. My scrapes were healing fast. For some inexplicable reason, Phoebe wore a khaki aviator's cap with earflaps along with her usual cat's-eye sunglasses. I tweaked the cap and slipped her thirty clams for the cab ride. She tried to give it back but I wouldn't let her.

Pinky and I hustled inside.

25

It was around dinnertime when our 747 coasted to a stop at the Minneapolis-St. Paul International Airport. We'd lost a couple of hours in the air. The mid-flight mystery chicken had been good enough for me, but Pinky was still hungry, so I whizzed her by the snack bar for a quick slice of pizza. It looked so good that I decided to get one, too. Afterwards, we cleaned up in the women's room and headed for the Thrifty rent-a-car counter.

Rush hour had pretty well subsided by the time we left the Crosstown Highway and headed north on 35W. It was weird. I'd been in Minneapolis less than a week ago, but the weather had turned drastically since then. Late summer splendor had changed to early fall chill. The flat horizon was a dreary, unbroken curtain of dark gray. A handful of buildings poked up from the downtown skyline like somebody's knuckles frozen in a hostile flourish.

I shivered and closed the window of the tinny Geo

Metro. Pinky was craning her neck every which way. She loved it here.

Pinky had agreed ahead of time to hang out at her Aunt Grace's while I conducted my business. I'd had no trouble convincing her—I knew Pinky had a bit of a crush on her cousin Gaitland. What she didn't know, at least not yet, was that Gaitland was gay. He was a few years older than Pinky, a hellion of a kid who played bass in a garage band that wanted to be the next Hüsker Dü. Grace had called me in a panic awhile back when she discovered well-thumbed copies of Jean Genet and James Baldwin among his books. I told her it could have been a lot worse. He could have been reading David Leavitt.

Pinky talked me into a detour on the way to Grace's. She wanted to stop at her favorite record store, Oar Folkjokeopus on Lyndale Avenue. That was okay by me. It would give me a chance to reorient myself to Christa Lovett's neighborhood.

We rolled off the freeway and turned left onto Lake Street, a main thoroughfare that bisects Minneapolis from east to west. This part of Lake had undergone a lot of changes since my college days a decade and a half ago. Once a scuzzy, comfortable strip of pool halls and liquor stores, the street was now a spiffed-up corridor of fast food outlets and chain stores. I kept my eyes peeled for a Budget Barn. Nope. On Pinky's urging, I drove around the block to the intersection of Lake and Hennepin. Here, in the heart of Uptown, I also noticed signs of a facelift. A mall, for chrissakes, and a bevy of Pinky Fury knockoffs cruising the streets in Doc Martens and hair the color of tropical sea creatures.

We drove up Hennepin and cut over on 28th Street.

Then, turning north onto Lyndale, I started checking the street numbers. It seemed Christa Lovett lived further up the road towards downtown. I dropped Pinky outside Oar Folk —a classic indie music shop that had survived a fire, blizzards, *and* the death of the record album—and kept heading north. There it was.

Just past the Wedge food co-op, I spotted Lovett's alleged address on a brown, wooden, two-story house with a wraparound porch. I circled the block and drove by once more. The house appeared to be divided into four apartments—at least I thought I saw four doorbells aligned by the front entrance. Two cars sat in the rutted driveway, a purple VW bug and a shiny late-model Honda Civic hatchback. The porch was ringed by a verdant assortment of shrubs and flowers. Everything seemed so wholesome here, it was hard to imagine Tucker Myles and her cohorts holed up inside. Maybe they weren't. But I was banking that—one way or another—Christa Lovett could at least steer me in the right direction.

I hightailed it back down Lyndale, smiling when I passed the Red Dragon restaurant. I had a lot of memories wrapped up in that little dive. I found Pinky leaning against the wall outside Oar Folk, a package clutched in her paw. She looked so…cool. So independent. I embarrassed her with a big show of affection, then hustled her into the rental heap.

Grace lived in an impossibly scenic, squeaky-clean neighborhood over by Lake of the Isles. It was getting dark, the air laced with a steady chill, but there they were, the healthy Minnesotans! They were out in force—biking, running, rollerblading, baby stroller-pushing, anything to get around the lake multiple times. There was a kind of Sisyphean madness to the whole thing. It made me tired just to watch them.

When we pulled up to my sister's house, Gaitland saun-tered out to greet us. At the moment, he was sporting a dec-imated Keith Richards look. I noticed, however, that he complemented the get-up with a set of multi-hued Freedom Rings around his neck, the latest in gay iconographic fash-ion. Pinky was in for a revelation.

I dispatched a round of kisses, then left them all to their devices. Back on Lyndale, I parked a block away from Lovett's and walked up to the front of the house. Oddly, the doorbells weren't labeled, so I risked irritating the neighbors and punched the top one first. No answer. I tried the second one. I heard footsteps, then a door to my left opened about six inches. A shaggy-haired woman said, "Yeah?"

"I'm looking for Christa Lovett. Do you know which apartment is hers?"

The woman pushed the screen door wider and I noticed a squirming tot in her arms. "Yeah. It's right over there." She pointed to the other end of the porch. "But I haven't seen her all week."

"Huh."

"You a friend?"

"Uh…business colleague."

"Hmm. Well, Christa's gone a lot on business. You probably know that." The baby suddenly squealed. "Shush," the woman said, giving the kid a little bounce.

I gestured at the driveway. "Is one of those her car?"

"Nope. She doesn't have one." Slight frown. "I don't think so, anyway."

I dallied, wondering what else I could glean from her. Hmm. I said, "Ma'am, is Christa, uh, single as far as you know? Does she have regular friends who come by?"

176

Shaggy Hair cocked her head. "What do you wanna know *that* for?"

"Oh, ah, her friends at the phone company are a little worried about her. They say she's real secretive about personal things."

The baby hiccuped, then commenced gurgling. The woman bounced it some more. "Well, that's for sure. I didn't even know she worked for the phone company." She turned to go in, then said, "And about your other question—" She shrugged broadly and retreated.

"Thank you," I called after her.

I walked over to Christa's door and knocked hard. Nothing. I had a creepy *deja vu* sensation, but fought it back and knocked again. I waited. Then I took a step sideways and peered in her front windows. The curtains were open, but in the deepening dusk all I could see were the shadowy outlines of furniture and what looked like a fireplace. Nothing extraordinary. I walked around the porch to the side of the house and found another door that apparently led into the back of Christa's apartment.

Over here, tree branches came down and swept the edge of the porch rail, partially shielding me from the street. I took a quick glance around, but didn't see anyone looking my way. My eyes must really be losing their keenness. Because as I dug my picklocks out of my pocket, a figure popped out of the darkness and clasped a cool hand across my mouth.

I tried to twist fast and aim a knee in the groin. But the hand, and the arm attached to it, was too strong. The other arm grabbed my wrist and jammed it into my back. I kicked down at the wooden planks of the porch, trying to arouse Shaggy Hair or some other neighbor. But the assailant dragged me quickly towards the back and down to the ground through a spot where the porch railing had rotted loose. I could only see the sleeve of a navy—blue windbreaker, but I smelled the ripe scent of sweat, the kind that comes from fear. I was pulled across the grass and into what seemed like a back alley, then shoved against the rough siding of a garage. It was hard to breathe. I willed myself to stem a tide of panic.

The hand loosened a bit and I sucked air between the fingers. Then I felt hot breath alongside my ear, and I started freaking again. A voice said, real softly, "Lady. I'm not going to hurt you. Just relax."

Yeah, right, buddy. I dragged some more oxygen and groped wildly for a way to attack. But my wrist was still pinioned, my chest and cheek pressed hard against the wall.

The man said, "Okay. We're goin' in the car. Just keep your goddamn mouth shut and I'll move my hand."

He started to pull away and, of course, I yelled as loud as I could. Slam! I was mashed against the garage again, more roughly this time, his now-clammy hand back across my mouth. He swore and pulled me towards a four-door sedan. Then he shoved me in the back seat and got in, too, forcing me down on my front.

This time when he moved his hand I couldn't shout; I was choking, gasping for air, a sense of dread edging me close to hysteria. The fellow fished around and found some rope on the floor of the car. When he turned back to tie my wrists, I craned to see his face. Jesus. He had a boomerang scar on his cheekbone and gold eyes shining brightly in the semi-darkness, like a cat's.

I stopped struggling. This was no random assault. This was the guy from the Cathedral Hill Hotel—the one I'd seen twice before. And now he was lurking a third time in the vicinity of Christa Lovett. I tried to think, but Yellow Eyes was hurting my arms as he tugged them behind me.

I said: "Don't tie me up."

"*What?*"

"Just…talk to me. I won't run."

He made an ugly sound. But he pulled me upright and looked me full in the face, still pinning my arms.

"What do you want?" I asked quietly. My jaw was sore and my cheek throbbed from its close encounter with the garage wall.

"We want to know what *you* want."

My mind shifted gears, but I couldn't figure this out. "Who's 'we'?"

Yellow Eyes scowled at me. He was a mean-looking man, cold and humorless. "'We' is none of your business. We know your name, we know you're some kind of snoop. What do you want with Lovett?"

"Look." I was starting to feel real angry. "The question is, what do *you* want with her? I saw you in San Francisco. I—"

"Fuck." He shoved me down and started groping in my clothes.

"Hey!" I kicked him in the chest, but my angle was all wrong and he lunged forward and caught me again as I scrambled for the far door. I gasped, "What the hell are you doing?"

"Patting you down, goddammit." He was breathing hard now, too.

"Jesus. I'm not carrying." I lifted my arms to get it over with, then cringed as he ran his hands over my body. He seemed satisfied. I crossed my arms over my chest and fixed him with a nasty glare.

I asked: "How did you know Christa Lovett's address?"

He snorted. "I followed you, lady. I've been on your tail since Lovett left Frisco. I was on the plane with you and the kid."

Shit—how'd I let that happen? I stared and repeated, "What do you want with her?"

Our *tête-à-tête* might have gone on indefinitely if Yellow Eyes hadn't taken some initiative. He tied my hands after all, but in front, loosely. Then he whipped out a big bandanna to use as a blindfold. That scared me a lot, but I took deep, even breaths as he secured it in place. Then he said we were going for a ride.

Ha. I could've guessed that. I just hoped it didn't culminate with cement shoes and a visit to one of Minnesota's 10,000-plus lakes.

I tried to pay attention, but after several turns and a few curving streets I had no idea where we were. We seemed to get on a highway—our speed increased and the pace stayed steady. Yellow Eyes never spoke. It could have been thirty minutes later, maybe forty, when I heard the car crunch to a stop on what sounded like a gravel roadway. My captor got out, opened the back door, and pulled me out of the vehicle. The air was brisk and clean; I detected the fresh, piney smell of the outdoors.

I guess the man had had a gun all along. I felt something cold and hard poke into my side. He told me to walk, guiding me up a short step and through what seemed like a doorway. Inside, it was way too warm, the air baking with the scratchy heat of an electric radiator. I caught another familiar scent. I sniffed deeply but couldn't place it.

I was escorted up two flights, the stairs narrowing as we

reached the top. My feet sank into what felt like shag carpet. Yellow Eyes pushed me into a room and closed the door behind us. The scent intensified. As he laboriously unfastened my blindfold, it struck me—Ambush.

The bandanna fell. Right before me at a desk, hammering away at an old Underwood typewriter, was Christa Lovett. I don't know which one of us was more surprised.

26

Lovett shot to her feet, throwing daggers at my chauffeur with her pretty gray eyes.

"What the *fuck* are you doing?" she snarled.

He remained silent, clearly pissed. I watched them stare each other down and took a gander at my surroundings. We were in a mid-sized attic room with slanted, insulated walls, brown shag carpet , and no other furniture besides the rickety desk. One window at the far side of the room was covered by brown wooden shutters. I started to sidle that way. "Hold it!" Yellow Eyes thundered.

I turned. He was pointing a silver-barreled piece in my direction. I wondered if that's what a 9mm Beretta looked like. I squinted—I didn't think so. He held it dead still as Lovett stormed over and stood right beside him, shouting into his face like a marine drill sergeant: *"Put the gun away!"*

He complied, but he didn't back off. Suddenly, I realized

what was wrong with this picture. Lovett was a new woman: her hair was chopped into a modified bowl cut and dyed the color of red clay, and her clothing consisted of ill-fitting blue jeans and a kelly-green rugby shirt. Quite a different effect from her smart retro lady's attire. Huh.

Lovett said to Yellow Eyes: "Get out of here. I want to talk to her, alone."

"I can't leave you two—"

"Well, why did you bring her here in the first place?" Lovett planted her fists on her hips.

"*You* got her into it," he protested. "Not me."

"Yeah, and I got her out of it. Now—"

"Bullshit. How the hell do you know what she's up to?"

Lovett dropped her jaw. "You think she's FBI?"

He heaved his shoulders in a sarcastic snit. "Uh-huh, maybe. I followed her to your old apartment. Whaddaya think she was doing there?"

She chuckled in a sad sort of way and turned to look at me. Her face seemed weary now—her muscles slack, her skin without luster. "She's not with the Feds," Lovett said, but there was a slight hesitation in her voice.

"Hey," I said. If I wasn't so tense, I might have laughed. "I'm private, remember? That's it. Besides"—I tried to muster some bravado—"*I'm* the captive here. I ought to be asking about you guys."

Christa said, again, "Leave us alone."

This time Yellow Eyes obeyed. He stormed out the door after issuing a stern directive to me to stay away from the window. I refrained from saluting. When he was gone, Lovett walked over and hugged me. I wasn't feeling that affectionate.

She fingered my cheek. "Did he hurt you?"

"Oh." I reached up a hand and worked my jaw around a little. "Just…mentally."

"I'm sorry."

"Listen." I put a few feet between us and sat down on the shag carpet. "Let's get to the point."

"Okay."

"Well?" I asked.

"Well…why did you come to Minneapolis?"

"To find you." Then I really did laugh. I'd found her all right, but this wasn't quite how I'd pictured it. "Christa, what's going on?"

She sat in her desk chair and sighed. "I can't tell you."

"Oh, come on. I'm assaulted, blindfolded, dragged here against my will…what? You guys are going to kill me?" I didn't really believe that, but I felt like getting the issue out on the table right away.

"Oh, no. Nell, I'm sorry. Mar—" She stopped herself. "He shouldn't have done that. He's turned into such an asshole."

"Ha. He didn't used to be?"

She shook her head but didn't elaborate.

"Why was he following me?"

"He was following *me*," she said. "When I, ahhh…left San Francisco he must have stayed on to figure out what you were doing."

"But why?"

Lovett looked away.

"Christa?"

"Believe me, I was pissed, too. He had no right—"

"Okay. He's an asshole, he had no right. So why are you holed up with him in this place?"

She blustered, "I'm not! It's just…temporary."

I changed course fast, while I still had the upper hand. "Christa, why did you leave San Francisco? Without telling me? Did you talk to Ellen?"

"No." Her voice was pained. "No. After Philip Gold died, I figured it was pointless. I couldn't do anything for Ellen without…"

"Without what?"

"Nothing. I just couldn't do anything more."

"Did you stop in Denver on the way back?"

Lovett blanched. "What?!" She banged her hand down, missing the table and striking the keyboard instead. A few letters flew up and jammed near the typewriter cartridge. She swore and dirtied her fingers trying to unjam them. Finally she blurted, "I didn't go to Denver! How do you know about that?"

I shrugged. "It seems we both have some secrets." I stood up and walked over to Christa. "Listen, I'm looking for Tucker Myles. She's Ellen's lover now—did you know that?"

"Yeah," Christa said, her eyes hardening. "I found out."

"A woman I know was shot over the weekend. I still don't know if she's gonna make it." I was starting to feel real surly. "I think Tucker Myles did it. I think she and Ellen, and maybe Rosie, are on the run. Everybody thinks the kidnapping was a fake."

I told Christa Lovett what I knew about Gold's deal with Budget Barn and what I surmised about the Myles/Norway extortion plan. As I was talking, I thought about my blindfolded ride, Lovett's change in appearance, this seemingly secluded house, and Yellow Eyes' paranoia. I decided to bet the farm.

"Christa, were you with Amanda McCracken when she

had a baby in Gary, Indiana? A baby girl named Rose?"

Lovett knocked her chair over as she stood up in a frenzy and backed away, her hands gripping her skull. Her eyes bored into me, frantic and wild.

"Whoa," I said, stretching an arm gently forward. "It's okay. I'm not going to tell anybody. I just need your help to find Tuck—"

"No!" she wailed. "You don't get it. *I'm* Amanda McCracken. Rosie's *my* child!"

Suddenly she was on the floor sobbing seventeen years' worth of tears. I was next to her, holding her tight, watching the whole scenario fall into place in my head like the unseemly footage of one hell of an unsolved mystery.

After we regained our equilibrium, Christa blindfolded me, escorted me to the bathroom, and led me outside to the car. I heard other voices as we passed through the house, along with Christa's raw one demanding the car keys from Yellow Eyes. The bandanna stayed on all the way back to town. We talked the whole time. It seemed Amanda McCracken had had a lot of aliases in her almost twenty years as a fugitive. Her recent one originated from her admiration for Christa Wolf, a writer from the former East Germany. Lovett? She'd never heard of Lyle, she just liked the sound of Lovett.

The mention of Lyle got me thinking. I asked Christa to join me for a nightcap at Lyle's, a chaotic little dive on Hennepin with a Fifties exterior, a Seventies interior, and a Twenties soul. We took a booth in the back. By the time we finished our first round of Leinenkugel beers, I'd heard the whole story and Christa was starting to get edgy. I was surprised at her emotional resilience, but then, Amanda McCracken had been toughing things out for quite some time. I was also surprised that she spoke so freely. I just coaxed her along, as empathic as I could be.

McCracken was indeed one of the Jersey 5, and Yellow Eyes was another. The other two survivors were both doing time on conspiracy charges unrelated to the original bombing. One woman was at Marianna, Florida; the other was at Lexington. McCracken had successfully evaded capture by hopping from town to town and job to job, though she'd been Christa Lovett, loyal phone company worker, for over five years. Now, with all the upheaval, she'd have to move on again.

McCracken had also been alone since her lover Ellen Norway, a fellow student and rabble-rouser, had left her. Apparently, Norway couldn't handle the pressure of going underground with McCracken. By then, McCracken was pregnant, the result of coerced sex with another politico.

"He raped you?" I asked quietly.

"Yeah." Lovett's knuckles were white as she strangled the neck of her beer bottle. "But I didn't think of it that way at the time. We were all supposed to lay back and take it."

McCracken decided to keep the baby, hoping somehow that she and Ellen and the kid could stay together. But that wasn't in the cards. Before Rosie was born, Ellen split. Then McCracken had a close call with the law and had to leave the country for a while. She contacted Ellen and asked her to keep Rosie, just for a bit. The time had stretched to seventeen years; Rosie had grown up thinking Ellen was her mother.

McCracken kept hoping they could all reunite, and she

could tell Rosie the real story. But Ellen grew increasingly uncommunicative over the years. When McCracken heard she was marrying a man, she freaked out.

"Damn," I said.

Christa bobbed her shorn head. "So I came to San Francisco and—what do you know—she had a woman lover after all."

"And that guy followed you because—?"

"Jesus, I don't know why. He thinks I'm obsessed with Rosie. I guess I am, but hell, I'm not going to blow our covers. Not after all this time."

"So he was just keeping tabs on you?"

"Yeah. Asshole."

I guffawed. Then I remembered Lovett's plane ticket. "But you were planning to stop in Colorado? To see Rosie?"

"Possibly, depending on what I found out in San Francisco. I figure she's old enough now to understand everything. Well, maybe not to *understand*, but at least to know what really happened."

Lovett peeled the corner of her label. She got some paper caught under her nail and fussed with it for a minute. When she continued, I got another hit of the bottomless sorrow she concealed with her pragmatic words. "Rosie may never want to see me. She might be furious when she finds out. I don't know. But I want to give her the option." She blew out a ragged sigh. "If I ever get a chance."

"Are you still going to try and contact her?"

"Yeah, but...not till things blow over. With Ellen."

"Aren't you worried?"

She looked at me blankly. "Of course."

I put my hand over her fidgeting fingers. "Christa, I think Rosie's with Ellen and Tucker. You don't have any idea where they are?"

She flipped her palm and slid her hand into her lap. "No."

"Why would they come to Minneapolis?"

Christa frowned. "They wouldn't come here. I don't think. Not while I'm around." Her eyes were wet.

"Are you sure?"

"No, but I'm pretty sure. I can't imagine it."

Damn. Both Tony Rodriguez and the Budget Barn VP had steered me halfway across the continent. For what, a wild-goose chase? All I could think was that Tucker Myles had deliberately misled both of them. Unless Tucker and Ellen planned to shepherd Rosie to her biological mom before dropping out of sight. Hmm—not likely.

I had another question, but I didn't know how to ask it without sounding naive. I tried anyway. "Christa, couldn't you come forward now, after all this time? Try and get amnesty or something?"

She tipped her bottle and fixed me with a solemn stare on the way back down. "Uh-uh. I'm still wanted on a fugitive warrant. Conspiracy, accessory to murder—whatever else they cooked up. I wouldn't stand a chance."

"So…" I was at a loss. "Can you get any work done anymore? I mean, political work?"

For the first time, I saw a trace of martyrdom in her melancholy smile. "I write articles under pseudonyms. Dole out advice. It doesn't amount to much. And it all seems so hopeless now, anyway.…" She swept an arm across the room, as if the motley denizens of Lyle's were responsible for all the war and hunger and poverty that marked these dreary times.

I knew what she meant, though. I drained my Leinie and felt a wave of near despair ripple through my guts. I excused myself and got up to use the bathroom, taking time to read the graffiti. When I returned, Christa was ready to call it a night. But she had one more thing to tell me.

"I'm sorry about your friend," she said evenly. "I hope she's okay. And I hope you find Myles. If you see Rosie"—she cast her eyes about the overly bright barroom—" Keep track of her whereabouts, will you? I may call you sometime."

I nodded tentatively.

We parted outside on the sidewalk. My rental car was just a few blocks away. The night air felt cold and clear, a spray of stars fanning out above us like pinpricks of white glitter. I watched as the proud, solitary figure of Amanda McCracken slid into her car, fired the engine, and disappeared into the flow of traffic streaming down Hennepin Avenue. I wondered what I'd say to Rosie Norway if I ever laid eyes on her again.

27

Grace Dickinson Fury was waiting up for me when I got to the house. She met me at the door with the latest Kat Colorado mystery glued to her hand, one finger curved to mark her place. At least we had some tastes in common.

She told me the kids were asleep. Then she peppered me with questions about my bruises, my quick trip to Minneapolis, my latest case, blah, blah, blah. Grace meant well, but I was too exhausted to explain much. Not that I could have anyway. I let her attend to my wounds, though, which seemed a little tender after all.

Grace was four years my senior, divorced, and a buyer for Dayton's department store. Women's dresses. We'd been tight growing up; in fact, I'd followed in her footsteps by going to school in Minneapolis. But years and miles had had their impact. So had our parents' deaths. Rather than drawing us closer, both instances had wedged us further apart, removing one more bond we shared in this lifetime.

Now Grace and I were polite and cautious, eyeing each other over a gulf that only seemed to deepen with time. It made me sad when I thought about it, which, frankly, wasn't very often.

Shoot. Maybe Grace and Harry and I should have a sibling reunion. Just the three of us, taking in a show at Vegas or something. What a concept.

I was stealing away to the guest room when Grace remembered to tell me Phoebe had called. Hmm. I looked at Elvis. He was still on California time—9:30 p.m. I thanked my sister, who headed off to bed. Then I scurried to the kitchen and punched Phoebe's number.

"Nellie," she said. Her voice was tense.

"Hi, Phoebes."

"I thought you should know—" She swore, then yelled to someone, "Just a sec! I'm on the phone." When she got back on the line, she said, "Jesus."

"What's wrong?"

"Nothing. Listen, there's this thing going on…have you found that woman Myles?"

"No."

"Well, you might want to get back here. I think she might be mixed up in this thing—"

"What?"

"A hostage stand-off."

"*What?!*" I was beginning to sound like a broken record.

"Some guy is holding hostages," Phoebe explained. "At a restaurant on Van Ness. Bull's. You know it?"

"Sure." Shit.

"He's got a couple of waitresses, and a manager, I think, and a kid—"

"What does this have to do with Myles?"

"The guy says he killed Philip Gold. Only he says it was self-defense."

"Damn." I thought Leonard Galle or somebody else from Budget Barn had iced Gold. "Who *is* this guy?"

"What's his name...oh, god, let me check...." Phoebe dropped the phone. I bit my lip until she came back a while later. "Raphaelson. Stan Raphaelson. He worked with Gold. He's—"

"—an Arts Commissioner."

"Yeah, how'd you know?"

"It doesn't matter. Is this on the news, or what?"

"Uh-huh. All the local stations are down there, live."

I thought fast. "How long has this been going on? What does Raphaelson want?"

"It started a couple of hours ago. I guess he pulled a gun on some kid, then let everybody go except her and a few of the staff. The cops are talking to him. He wants immunity in exchange for some damaging evidence against Budget Barn."

"Oh, my god."

"Yeah. It's a little confusing. All the stations have slightly different versions."

"Well, what are the cops doing?"

"I think they agreed to the demands. But now the guy's freaking out —I guess he realizes the cops are just *saying* that. At least that's what it seems like. Now it's a stand-off."

I rested my forehead against the wall of Grace's kitchen. The wallpaper was blurry up close, its little pink-and-yellow floral vines swimming around like amoebas under a micro-scope. I'd really screwed things up. Actually, I hadn't done anything—I'd been traipsing around one step behind all the action. Well, at least I knew that whatever happened with

195

Stan Raphaelson, I'd already blown the whistle on Budget Barn.

Why would Raphaelson have killed Philip Gold? I suppose he would've been pissed if he found out about Gold's scam. But why this extreme behavior now?

I blew out some air. Why did anyone do anything? Sometimes you could figure it: I thought of horrific hate crimes, like the Montreal massacre of women engineering students, or the kids in Maine who threw a gay man off a bridge. Jesus. But why shoot up a random McDonald's? Why pull a gun on a kid at Bull's…

I said, "Phoebe, who's the kid?"

"What?" She'd drifted off, too. I guess she had her eyes peeled to the tube.

"The kid. Do they know who it is?"

"You mean in Bull's? The hostage?"

"Yeah."

"No, I don't think so—"

"Do they have a description?" I asked.

"Uhhh." She paused. "She's a teenager, blonde—"

"Ponytail?"

"Yeah."

"Kind of trim? Athletic?"

"Uh-huh. I think so."

Rosie Norway. Raphaelson was holding Rosie Norway.

"Phoebes, I'm coming home."

"Good."

"Will you do me a favor? Call the cops. Tell 'em it's probably Ellen Norway's daughter."

"The kid?!"

"I think so. Do it anonymously, if you want."

"Oh, Nell…"

After we hung up, I called the airlines. The next flight to San Francisco wasn't until 5 a.m. Given the time zones, that would still get me in at an early hour. I changed my ticket, then reconfirmed Pinky's midday flight to New York, with a transfer to London. Afterwards, I found a bottle of Scotch in Grace's cabinet and took a belt.

I wanted to spend a little more time with Pinky, but it was the dead of night. What the heck. First I showered and put on my one clean shirt with the same old gray pants. My eyeballs were shot with red, my face so puffed and green on one side that it looked like a bruised honeydew melon. I practiced smiling. It wasn't very convincing. I combed my wet curls into the approximation of a hairdo, packed my bag, then went to wake up Pinky.

She was a good sport. Or maybe she was too sleepy to register that I was leaving more than a few hours ahead of schedule. She asked about the bruise. I spun a vague tale, realizing as I spoke that I wasn't going to tell anybody—not a soul—about Amanda McCracken. Pinky and I sipped coffee and killed the next few hours together until it was time for me to go. I made a promise to myself that I'd visit London that winter, no matter what.

I made sure Pinky had her plane tickets. Then I started worrying, but she assured me Gaitland would get her to the airport on time. I asked her to kiss her aunt and cousin goodbye for me. As I gathered my things, Pinky disappeared for a moment. She came back with a sheaf of loose papers collected in an old-fashioned cardboard notebook, the kind that tied with a string.

"Here, Mum." Pinky blushed.

I took the notebook.

"It's stuff I've been doing," she said, "you know, over

the summer."

Wow. Pinky Fury poetry. First editions.

"Thanks, honey," I whispered, then smothered her in a farewell embrace.

As I tooled off in the Geo Metro, the sun was beginning its cyclical fight with the skyline. It cast a pink-orange glow above the flat Minnesota horizon like a dose of pastel food coloring poured down from the heavens.

28

I was planning to take a cab, but when I stumbled through the sliding glass doors of the airport terminal, a Quake City Shuttle was revving its engine right there, as if by fate. I knew a maniacal Quake City driver would get me home as fast as any cabbie, and save me an Andy Jackson, to boot. I flagged down the shuttle, hopped aboard, and buckled in for the ride. The radio was busted, but the bald driver with the cobra tattoo on his skull told me he thought the hostage thing was still going on.

When I got home it was 7:15 a.m. I ran upstairs to dump my stuff and use the bathroom. I flicked on the radio and found a news update. The stand-off was in its eleventh hour. The police were sitting tight, waiting for Raphaelson to pass out from exhaustion. The restaurant manager and a waitress had been released. Now it was just the other waitress and the teenager, the latter tentatively identified as Rosie Norway, daughter of the woman kidnapped last week. Hmm. The cops were keeping mum on their suspicions.

I tore off my clothes and opted for maximum comfort: black jeans, an old Loveless Motel T-shirt, and the hightop Keds. I grabbed a jacket and sprinted back downstairs. The reliable ragtop was resting peacefully at the curb. It sported more grime, a spreading patch of rust and—I noticed with chagrin—a parking ticket. I'd forgotten about Tuesday morning street cleaning. I plucked it from the wiper and stuffed it in my pocket. Then I opened the top and lit out for Dodge.

One thing was bugging me. If Rosie really was being held at gunpoint by a crazed fanatic, where was Ellen Norway? Wouldn't she come out of hiding for her adopted daughter's sake, if nothing else? Could she be that cold-hearted? Maybe she and Myles really had left town. In which case, how had Rosie ended up with Raphaelson? I couldn't believe she just happened to be dining at the very restaurant where her mother's fiancé's murderer decided to flip his lid.

I was confusing myself. I careened down Dolores, figuring I'd keep an eye peeled for Norway and Myles when I scoped out the scene at Bull's. Traffic was jammed up where Dolores met Market. When I could finally turn right, I noticed a road crew blocking off lanes where Market Street ran underneath a highway overpass. Damn.

I siphoned into the one open lane and crawled along. When I passed beneath the highway, I saw a couple of gaffer's trucks and other movie company paraphernalia taking up space, along with a crowd of women in habits. Great. Another traffic snafu, courtesy of Hollywood. I swore and kept inching forward. The tension was making me sweat. I shrugged off my jacket and tossed it into the back seat.

Then I noticed an open meter in the block before the Zuni Cafe. I flipped a U across Market, no mean feat at the height of rush hour. I backed into the space, offered up some coins to the parking gods, and trotted off in the direction of Van Ness Avenue. I could see traffic snarled up that way, too. The streets around Bull's were probably all cordoned off.

I paused when I got within a block of the commotion. What did I think I was going to do that the SFPD Tactical Unit couldn't do? Or all the other muscle no doubt swarming around?

I kicked myself. Don't be so modest, Fury. What would Kinsey do? For one thing, Kinsey would have a gun, I thought glumly. But heck, I'd made peace with myself on the issue—I wasn't going to start packing now.

Bull's was a big, ballsy, Texas kind of joint that anchored the ground floor of a beautifully restored building near the foot of Van Ness. Arched windows rose two stories high around the base of the white stone structure, with doors on two sides leading into the wood-panelled restaurant. Smart neon signs advertised the place, the two "L"s of Bull's shaped into jaunty cowboy boots. It was popular with attorneys, politicians, and other drones who wandered in from the many neighboring office buildings. Popular, too, with those who fancied a nice, bloody steak every now and then.

Upstairs from the restaurant, the building housed a number of city agencies, including the San Francisco Arts Commission. I wondered if Stan Raphaelson planned this episode, or if he just moseyed down for happy hour and fell prey to a bout of panic. When I got abreast of the situation, I spied flapping yellow police streamers and wooden barricades blocking the streets on four sides. A whole slew of armed personnel was positioned around the perimeter of the building, some even hunkered down on the roof of Zim's Restaurant across the street. Reporters and TV mini-cams were on the scene, as were plenty of curious onlookers. Everybody looked haggard, except for a zealous few who were lapping up the excitement. It could've been a scene right out of *Dog Day Afternoon*, except instead of desperate, love-whipped Al Pacino, a heretofore unremarkable bureaucrat was the one calling the shots. I felt kind of queasy.

At first I didn't recognize any of the cops or bystanders. I didn't see Princess, either, though I figured she'd be here. The thought made me nervous. Then I saw a familiar helmet of silver hair atop an angular figure: Meg Halliway.

I walked toward her, knowing better than to offer a hug. Instead, I placed a gentle hand on her forearm and asked about her lover and my pal, Lydia Luchetti. Meg said she was out of the woods and on her way to a full recovery—there was no permanent brain damage.

I grinned and hugged Meg after all; she responded with a tight smile. I was starting to pump her for further details when another recognizable form sidled up beside me. Tad Greenblatt.

He nodded congenially at Halliway, then turned to me.

"Whatcha doing here, kiddo?" he asked.

"Tad." I elbowed him. "Lydia's going to be all right!"

Greenblatt was dressed for eighteen holes, not for a hostage crisis—spotless polo shirt, peppermint-striped seersucker suit, white bucks. He looked good enough to eat. As if on cue, my stomach growled loud enough to turn a few heads. I realized I hadn't had anything to eat since a slice of pizza about a million years ago.

I pointed at Bull's and said: "What's the latest?"

A whir of helicopter blades drowned out his answer. I

saw him gesture with his left hand toward Bull's, then down Oak Street, which ran along the side of the building. Suddenly there was a lot of movement and a bark of rapid-fire instructions spewing from a bullhorn. Halliway darted away in the direction of a knot of cops.

Tad said something else, but I missed that too. Out of my peripheral vision, I caught a flurry of motion on the Zim's roof. I turned to see the SWAT guys drop into position, rifles pointed at Bull's. As I whirled back around, Tad tried to yank me down to the sidewalk, but I stubbornly squirmed out of reach. Suddenly everything was happening at once. All eyes were focused on a woman in a tan trench coat who had busted through a barricade and was tearing pell-mell towards the front of Bull's, an unmistakable glint of metal in her right hand.

"Fury!" Tad thundered.

But I was fixated. I scurried sideways, crab-like, trying to get a better vantage point. I'd only seen a few photos of Ellen Norway, but judging from the profile and hairline of the woman in tan, it was indeed her. She blasted inside, heedless of the bullhorned warnings. A report of gunfire rang out from Bull's. I sucked some air and watched a squadron of armed officers storm through the front doors. It was going down.

I jostled through the crowd to the foot of Oak Street. Moments later, one cop emerged from the front, a sheltering arm around a sobbing young woman—the waitress, I presumed. No Rosie, no Ellen. I heard shouting inside. Suddenly, Rosie's blonde head was visible at the side door. She stumbled all the way through, a tallish guy in an olive-green suit pinching her arm and pressing a gun barrel to the side of her head. Raphaelson. He pushed her along.

Someone yelled, "Hold your fire!" As Raphaelson started jogging down Oak Street, Rosie tripped. Rapaelson pulled at her viciously, forcing her to trot along with him. A swarm of law enforcers followed in their wake, keeping a cautious distance. Raphaelson veered hard to the left, apparently cutting through a parking lot that spilled onto Market Street.

I don't know what got into me. Maybe it was thoughts of Pinky, her poems that I read on the plane still fresh and raw in my mind. Or of Amanda McCracken and her seventeen years of heartache. Or maybe it was the Kinsey in me, gun-free but still up for a brawl. In any event, I whipped into action, sprinting away from the crowd and around the corner onto Market.

I was adjacent to the parking lot in no time. Rosie and Raphaelson had just passed through, and were running awkwardly in tandem in the direction of the Zuni Cafe. Stray pedestrians scattered when they saw the weapon glued to Rosie's head. I kept jogging. I was close enough to hear her gagging and gasping for breath. Now the cops were yelling at *me*, but I tuned 'em out, concentrated on the gun. I was waiting for Raphaelson to stumble or get distracted, anything that would cause him to lower the piece, if only for a second.

I got my chance when a delivery van barreled into the alley between the Zuni and the Red Desert cactus store and abruptly blocked their paths. Raphaelson faltered, looked wildly for an alternative, and inadvertently shifted his trigger arm. As the van squealed forward, I ran, dove, and knocked Raphaelson to the pavement with none of the grace of your average defensive tackle but, hey, it was good enough for me.

He landed with a thud. The impact sent the gun rocketing from his hand. It flew straight through the broad, plate-glass window of the Zuni Cafe, scattering liquor bottles, tumbling the fresh oyster cart, and no doubt surprising the tony patrons assembled inside for a spot of *petit dejeuner*. A shower of fine glass shards rained down upon us like a sudden hailstorm of precious gems.

As if that wasn't enough destruction for one day, I heard a resounding squeal of tires and raised my battered head in time to see a pickup truck race down Market Street, zoom off a movie set stunt ramp, apparently lose control in mid-air, and land upside down with a sickening splat on top of my beloved pale blue vintage Mustang convertible.

29

Tucker Myles was apprehended traveling north on Highway 5 when—of all things—she was forced to stop at a random sobriety checkpoint. An APB had been out on her since that morning when both Rosie Norway and Stan Raphaelson had confirmed police suspicions. Rosie said she thought Myles had shot Lydia Luchetti; Raphaelson said Myles tried to extort money from him after learning that he'd killed Philip Gold.

Raphaelson confessed readily, but reiterated that the killing was self-defense. He said he'd discovered doctored Arts Commission paperwork, followed Gold to the Budget Barn construction site after they both worked late that night, and accused Gold of accepting payoffs. They'd scuffled, then Raphaelson had defended himself with a brick when Gold went on a rampage.

Later, Budget Barn tried to coerce Raphaelson into filling Gold's shoes. Raphaelson balked, and stashed a gun in his desk at the office in case anyone else tried to push him around. He finally lost his cool when Myles stepped in with another demand of blackmail.

Meanwhile, Tucker Myles was admitting nothing, but a Budget Barn dossier that arrived mysteriously in Tuesday's mail linked her to a sweeping case of corporate fraud. Unless some behind-the-scenes wheeling and dealing exonerated Leonard Galle and his cohorts, Myles would go down with the lot of them. Plus, the gun that Ellen Norway used to storm Bull's was a 9mm Beretta, easily identified as the one registered to Myles. Apparently, Norway had swiped it when Myles refused to assist in Rosie's rescue. The two women had been squabbling, in fact, since Norway accused Tucker Myles of shooting Lydia Luchetti. At least that's what Rosie said.

I learned all of this and much, much more, during an extended session at the cop shop following my display of heroics back on Market Street. I'd pulled myself up from the wreckage with a new collection of cuts and bruises, nothing very serious. Rosie was hospitalized for observation, but she was going to be fine, too, at least physically. Ditto Raphaelson, who'd suffered a broken arm in the fall and was now freely blabbing to the cops, trying to buy himself leniency. Nobody was hurt too badly at the Zuni, either. In fact, the only person who wouldn't recover from the episode was Ellen Norway, who took a bullet in the chest during her confrontation with Raphaelson.

Before she died, Norway owned up to the fake kidnapping. As I suspected, she'd found out about Gold's arrangement with Budget Barn when she overheard a damning phone call. She figured she could pad her already plump pocketbook before leaving Gold for Tucker Myles, then the two of them could vanish underground. That was before Norway learned the full extent of Myles' deviousness. I may never know why Norway squealed on her deathbed, but chances are it had something to do with remorse over Lydia Luchetti and the whole sorry turn of events.

It took a call to the ace reporter herself to learn how she'd zeroed in on Tucker Myles before anyone else. Lydia Luchetti told me she was snooping at Norway's office and— after eavesdropping on a telephone call between Myles and Rodriguez—realized that a shakedown was going on. She got Myles' Oakland address from a previous landlord and headed over there that fateful night, figuring Myles had something to do with Gold's murder. It was a hunch that almost cost her her life.

Lydia was groggy, but happy to hear from me and to spill her story. Before signing off, I mentioned that now she owed *me* one. Luchetti guffawed. I felt enormously reassured.

I suppose I'll never figure out what Leonard Galle had in mind for Myles, but I suppose it didn't matter anymore. Everybody'd been using everybody else, and the end results weren't pretty. Lots of death, lots of heartache, lots of loneliness in store for the survivors: Rodriguez' woman friend, Norway's parents, Rosie, Amanda McCracken, and many others, I'm sure, who I didn't even know about.

Budget Barn mucky-mucks would surely be hauled on the carpet for their chicanery, but a local chain would probably materialize and prosper anyway. An overhauled Arts Commission would scramble to salvage its reputation and eventually regain its middle-of-the-road footing. The McCrackens of the world would continue their uphill struggles to make a difference, and usually suffer the wrath of an immovable society. Business as usual here in the big city.

For the second time in a week, I sought refuge in a police station bathroom. The harsh fluorescent lights made my face appear ghastly, more sallow than it really was. I surveyed the fresh abrasions on one cheek and down both forearms. I'd re-injured both palms, too, and torn holes in the knees of my jeans.

I'd already cleansed all the wounds, but my scraped knees had begun to bleed again. I bent over and dabbed at them with an industrial-strength paper towel as gentle as sandpaper. The grubby black-and-white tiles started swimming beneath my feet. I had to lean against the porcelain to regain my equilibrium.

That's how Tad Greenblatt found me, bent over the sink and wincing from the sting of my kneecaps. "Hey," I said, straightening and pointing at the door. "Don't you have any respect?"

"Sure. But I dole it out sparingly."

He came over and stood beside me, frowning down at my sloppy ministrations. I resumed dabbing. After a while Tad said, "Helluva thing. About your car."

"Helluva thing," I replied, but it felt like somebody else talking, my zombie twin perhaps.

"Nellie, you know the stunt driver's okay, don't you?"

"Yeah, I heard."

Tad made a noise. "I guess that's why they pay those suckers thirty thousand bucks a day."

The zombie chortled.

"A good thing they're insured up the ying-yang," Tad went on. "You'll get compensated. I mean, you can't re-place an old Mustang, but hell, get something new and zippy, a Probe maybe—"

"Tad," I said, interrupting his irritating display of optimism. "The car belonged to Cate Jones. Remember? She'll get the money."

"Well, sure, but she'll buy you something new. Why the hell not? She—"

"Drop it, will you Greenblatt? Cate's not going to buy me another car. Look what I did to the first one."

"*You* didn't do it."

I just tossed my head, impatiently raking back a sweaty hank of hair that was plastered to my forehead.

"Well, cheer your own goddamn self up," Tad retorted good-naturedly. Then he added, "There's something else...."

"What?"

"I talked to a production guy from that movie. It's some kind of nun crime caper, can you believe that shit? They want to offer you a little something, you know, for your trouble...."

I squinted at Tad. "Huh?"

"A part in the movie!"

"Oh god."

"Nellie, it's great. They're redoing the chase scene, since they fucked it up, only they're adding a motorcycle. They need someone to play a nun on a bike! No dialogue, just a scene where the nun drives down Market tailing the pickup—"

"*No way* , Greenblatt, are you nuts?!"

He grinned.

Then I cracked up. Maybe Tad fabricated the whole thing. I'll never know. He started laughing, too, and we kept howling until a cop with a full belt of hardware swaggered in and gave us a dirty look. We left the women's room and kept going down to the lobby and out the front door of 850 Bryant. The midday sun cast a false cheer upon the street lined with bail bondsmen, pawn shops, and hole-in-the-wall lunch spots that sent an odor of rancid grease wafting through the neighborhood.

My hunger pangs kicked in again. I asked Tad to join me for lunch. He said he was game. He also said he'd drive me over to Davies Medical Center after we ate. Rosie Norway wanted to talk to me today.

We settled on a restaurant in Hayes Valley. On the way there, I asked Tad why he'd been hanging around during the hostage stand-off. He was hush-mouthed about it, admitting only that business was slow and he'd had the time. I gave him a skeptical once-over, but he shrugged it off. Tad had arrangements with the SFPD that I'd never fully understand or condone. So far, at least, it hadn't interfered with our friendship.

Powell's is a chicken joint on Hayes Street, a longtime fixture trying to hold its own amidst the sudden proliferation of kitschy shops and galleries. We downed fried chicken, greens, and slabs of sweet-potato pie before motoring on to the hospital. Tad dropped me off outside the front entrance, and for the second time that day, I found myself fending off the hungry news media. It seems I was celebrity *du jour*. Hmm. Maybe I'd even top Joe Montana on the evening news.

30

Rosie Norway was lying on her side, pages of the *San Francisco Examiner* spread out across the hospital bed. The afternoon paper had successfully engineered a scoop. The Raphaelson incident was front and center; I noticed a prominent sidebar with my name in the headline. No mention of Budget Barn, though. I guess reporters hadn't had time yet to crack that nut.

Rosie looked up at me and tried to smile. Her lips looked bloodless, her already pale eyes even more colorless and sunk deep into a pair of shadowed sockets. Yup, I could see a trace of Amanda McCracken—that's what had haunted me from the start. A few fresh bandages adorned Rosie's face, and some nasty-looking bruises leaked out from the edges of her hospital gown. Her blonde locks were loose, falling in tangled clumps across the bedsheets.

I stepped closer and instinctively put a hand on her forehead. Then I jerked away, a little embarrassed, but Rosie didn't seem to mind. Again, she seemed so young to me, younger than Pinky. I pulled up a visitor's chair and took a seat. Rosie's smile had never quite materialized, and now it vanished entirely. I thought she might start crying.

"I'm so sorry about your mom," I said straight away.

Rosie nodded, then just stared at me solemnly.

"Have you been able to sleep?"

"Not really."

"Are they"—I glanced around the sterile, single room— "treating you okay?"

"Nell," she said slowly, ignoring my question. "Did you know my mom and that...that woman Tucker...did you know they were...together?"

I sighed. "Rosie, I never met your mom. But, yes, I heard they were...involved."

Rosie seemed more curious than upset. Suddenly, she gripped my hand and started speaking in a monotone. "She never had guys around, you know? I never even thought about it. The whole time I was growing up. Then she met Philip, but it was weird. They were so...boring together." Her grip tightened. "She started bringing Tucker home and I was so stupid—I didn't get it. I thought they were, like, best friends."

"It's okay," I said, trying to sound matter-of-fact. "I bet she would have told you about it. When she was ready."

"Yeah." Rosie smiled wanly. "It's no big deal, anyway. I mean, gay people are cool...."

I kept my mouth shut. Rosie reclaimed her hand and draped it across her eyes. I wondered if this was what she wanted to talk to me about. Or if there was something else as well. I said: "Rosie, you know when you called me the other day? Then backed off? What was going on?"

She sat up and leaned forward, arms crossed loosely over her knees. I remembered the hell she'd gone through in the last 24 hours, and realized she must be tougher than her fine frame suggested.

"My mom called," Rosie explained, cocking her head. "I guess it was Sunday morning. She told me she was okay, that she and Tucker were hiding out in a motel. They wanted me to join them. So I did. I don't know—it seemed so romantic. Like a movie."

I nodded. "And you didn't tell anyone? Mrs. Zimmer?"

"No. Mom told me not to."

"So where'd you go?"

"Ugh. This place downtown. It was at, like, Sixth and Mission. It was gross."

"Why were they hiding out?" I asked, even though I knew the answer.

"Tucker was in some kind of trouble. But they wouldn't tell me what it was. I didn't know she'd tried to kill somebody." Rosie glanced downward and scrunched up the bedsheet in two fists. "They wanted to blackmail that guy, you know, Raphaelson, and then leave town with all the money."

She added, almost proudly, "They were going to let me decide. I could have gone with them if I wanted to. Or not."

I smiled. "So they trusted you to keep their secret?"

"Yeah." Rosie's eyes got wet.

"What were you going to do?"

"I don't know. It was so—" She sniffled. "So wild. Then they started fighting. I don't know—"

"That's okay." I reached for a tissue on the bedside table and handed it to Rosie. She palmed it, letting her eyes brim over freely. I asked, "So what happened? With Raphaelson?"

She took a ragged breath. "Tucker asked me to bring him this note—it was a blackmail note, I guess. It was in a sealed envelope."

I tried to squelch my rage at Myles. It was tough.

Rosie went on, "Mom didn't want me to go, but I didn't mind. It seemed kind of exciting. I brought the note to his office, and I was just supposed to wait and bring back a reply. The guy asked me to go downstairs and have a Coke while he thought about it. He seemed so, I don't know, normal."

I nodded.

"So I waited at the restaurant. Then he came in with a gun, and—" She shrugged weakly. "You know what happened."

"I'm so sorry." I reached over to hug her. Rosie felt limp and pliable, like a Gumby.

She said through her sniffles, "Thanks Nell. I mean, for tackling him. The cops were so…slow."

"They just didn't want you to get hurt."

"But they didn't help my mom!" she wailed, suddenly letting the tears fly freely.

"I know, sweetie." I laid her gently back in the bed and waved away a nurse who was hovering in the doorway. Then I sat for a while, just keeping an eye on her heaving form.

So Ellen hadn't told her about her biological mom, Amanda McCracken. I guess I'd do as Amanda requested: keep in touch with Rosie in case Amanda ever wanted to try and contact her again. I wondered how Ellen's death would affect Amanda. I shook my head. Just another sad angle to this whole botched affair.

I stayed until Rosie Norway fell into a twitchy sleep. I

left my card on the table, with a note asking her to call when she felt like it. On my way out of Davies Medical Center, I ran into Mrs. Zimmer. She thanked me, too, and corralled me for a little chat. She told me Rosie eventually wanted to go back to school, but meanwhile, she'd always have a home at the Zimmers'. Well, that was one thing to be grateful for.

I dodged the reporters by sneaking out a side door. But I wasn't moving very quickly, my body stiff and creaky from all its recent trials. I was trying to remember where I'd parked the Mustang when a flood of mental images washed over me like scenes from a gruesome coming attraction—the inert, gasping figure of Lydia Luchetti, the agitated Amanda McCracken pacing her Minnesota attic, Tony Rodriguez tumbling doll-like through mid-air, and the window of the Zuni Cafe shattering into a myriad of silvery pieces.

Then I saw the convertible, a flat, metal pancake bleeding powder-blue hunks of wreckage. Oh yeah. *That's* where I'd parked the Mustang.

31

I pushed aside the little orange umbrella with my fore-finger, then lifted the hefty glass to my lips. A rainbow swirl of liquids floated near the top, a clear mass of crushed ice hung in the center, and a layer of deep brown rum anchored the base. It wouldn't have been my first choice of drink, but Phoebe had insisted I stick with the theme. So I'd ordered a hurricane, Phoebe a mai tai, and Tammie Rae Tinkers a lime-green frozen daiquiri. Johnnie Blue was supposed to be here, too, but she got called away at the last minute to audition in L.A.

"Wow," I'd said.

Phoebe had raised her brow and nodded sagely.

We were at the Tonga Room, a supremely tacky faux-Polynesian joint nestled in the bowels of the ritzy Fairmont Hotel at the top of Nob Hill. Tourists seemed to know about the place. In fact, whole busloads of heartland types wan-dered in to sip frou-frou drinks, nibble hors d'oeuvres, and sway around a dance floor shaped like the hull of a ship. Captains' wheels, rope netting, and buoys added to the nautical motif, and fake thatched huts sprouted up here and there. I was surprised they didn't hire Gilligan impersonators to work the room.

What they did have, though, was a spectacular pond in the center of the action, complete with a covered floating bandstand. A trio of grass-skirted musicians meandered back and forth across the water, crooning old standards like "Under the Boardwalk" and "Strangers in the Night." Periodically, movie-set thunder and lightning would crackle through the room, then a torrent of rain would gush down and pummel the bandstand roof like an overearnest sprinkler system gone awry. It killed me every time.

We'd come to the Tonga Room to toast Rae on the eve of her departure. Tomorrow morning, she'd load the back of her Bronco II and hit the road for Nashville. I twirled my umbrella and watched her out of the corner of my eye. Rae was dressed down tonight, wearing a pair of pajama-style pants with little paisley swirls and an oversized black V-neck sweater cut low enough to show some cleavage. She caught me looking and smiled broadly, her wet periwinkle eyes wide as quarters.

Crrrackkk! Just then, a bolt of cartoon lightning streaked across the ceiling. I sucked rum through a straw and looked over at the band as it broke into "New York, New York," the drummer executing some fancy fingerwork with her sticks.

That afternoon, Tammie Rae Tinkers had asked me to go with her to Nashville. Not to stay, just to go along for the drive. It was right after we had sex, a particularly frolicsome episode during which neither of us said anything remotely sentimental. When Rae popped the question, I declined automatically. It was true: my case had careened to a close, I'd squared things with my satisfied client, Henry Gravatt, and I had a chunk of leftover change. But I still needed to finish some paperwork, deal with the cops, find an office space, and drum up some new business. Not to mention solve my automobile dilemma. I just couldn't zip across the country at the drop of a hat. Not again.

Rae hadn't pushed it. We'd kissed some more and talked about everything but her impending trip. Now she was messing with my palm under cover of the table as Phoebe told us about a new women's band called Running With Scissors.

"'Running With Scissors'?!" I ran my fingertips along the inside of Rae's thigh. Her pants were unbearably soft, her leg solid and warm underneath.

"Yeah," Phoebe said, taking a hearty belt of mai tai. "Isn't that great? They ought to play a set with My Bloody Valentine."

"Phoebes," I said, bringing both hands back into public view. "What's with the hat?"

"Huh?"

I guffawed and reached over to nuzzle her new favorite thing, the khaki aviator's cap.

"Oh." Phoebe grinned. "You like it?"

Rae and I looked at each other and shrugged. Phoebe Grahame could wear anything and look as elegant as Audrey Hepburn, as rakish as Montgomery Clift. I said, "Sure, sweetheart, it's the real you."

"You guys," Phoebe said slowly, hooking her arms around the back of her chair. "I've got some news."

Crrrackkk! Kaboom! Pellets of rain coursed down on the pond, the bandstand drifting through with the calm grace of a swan. "What?" I said, over the racket.

"I'm going to flight school!" Phoebe shouted.

"Flight school?!"

"Yeah." She looked very pleased with herself. "I'm going to be a pilot."

The noise subsided. I gawked at my best pal and stammered, "What for?"

Phoebe laughed. "What do you mean, 'what for?' So I can fly, of course." She tugged an earflap. Suddenly she looked just like Amelia Earhart. I should have seen this coming. Phoebe hadn't been herself lately, not since someone poisoned her with notions about Saturn and its return.

"But..." I stumbled for words. "Isn't it dangerous?"

"Less dangerous than driving to the airfield."

I tried again. "Isn't it expensive?"

"Not really," she explained. "I can take ground class at a community college, then go in for group lessons with a flight instructor. There's a school out at the San Carlos Airport. A guy at the garage was telling me about it."

"What about your job?" I whimpered.

"Nellie, chill out! I'm going to keep driving for Barbary Coast. But maybe someday I'll be able to *fly* you around, too. And fly Johnnie to her shows...." Phoebe tripped out on an adventure fantasy while I shook my head and looked disbelievingly at Phoebe, at Rae, and at the whole surreal scene going down at the Tonga Room.

Rae stood up and kissed Phoebe's cheek. "I think that's great. I can't wait to ride shotgun." Then she walked over and huddled with the band as it bobbed alongside the ersatz ship railing.

I took a big slurp of hurricane and said to Phoebe: "What's Rae doing?"

Phoebe lifted her shoulders, then reached a hand across the table and nudged my arm. "Hey. Are you all right?"

I nodded, suddenly too choked up to talk.

"What? This flying thing? It's really safe, don't worry—"

"Oh, I know," I muttered miserably. "It's really cool, Phoebe. Congratulations." I leaned over and clinked my glass against hers disspiritedly.

"Are you upset about your case?" Phoebe asked quietly. "I know you never found Christa Lovett but, hell, you busted up Budget Barn and saved that kid, and the Arts Commission has to come clean now—"

"Phoebes." I forced a grin. "I'm fine, okay?" I lunged over and playfully snatched her cap, then tugged it down over my curls. I really was okay, at least for the moment. I was sitting in a damp bar sucking rum in Everybody's Favorite City, with Phoebe and Rae by my side and all my worries—and recent memories—on hold until tomorrow.

Phoebe smiled back and lifted her glass.

Then Rae was walking our way, her hips doing marvelous things inside the loose fabric of her pants. She sat down and joined us in a toast. "The song," she said. "It's for both of you."

The Tonga Room trio launched into "The Way We Were" as another crack of thunder jolted the room and a rainstorm poured down from the phony skies, as torrential as my stockpile of tears would be if I ever bothered to open the floodgates.

32

The next morning I awoke before sunrise, kissed Rae's sleeping hulk, and hustled home on foot. I quickly showered and threw together a bag of essentials—jeans, white T-shirts, a toothbrush, Pinky's poems, Fig Newtons, early Dwight Yoakum. Stuff like that. Then I left a message on Tad Greenblatt's office machine, asking him to stop by and feed Flannery and Carson from time to time.

I was back at Rae's by 7:00 a.m., just as she finished stuffing items into the rear of her off-white Bronco II. I threw my bag on top of the pile and said, "Where should we stop for lunch? Around Bakersfield? Or should we power on through to Barstow?"

"What?!" Rae's eyes started crinkling up.

"Road trip. You and me. To the Athens of the South." I threw my arms around Tammie Rae Tinkers and squeezed her blue.

Rae was all smiles. "Okay, Fury. But I'm picking the

music...."

We hopped aboard and pointed east. I kept my eyes front and center as we rolled away from San Francisco. There'd be plenty of time to look back.

Photo by Donna Tauscher

Elizabeth Pincus is an ex-private eye living in San Francisco. Her first novel, *The Two-Bit Tango,* was nominated for a Lambda Literary Award and is currently being adapted for the stage. Pincus is a film critic for the *SF Weekly* and at work on her next Nell Fury novel.

Other Titles Available From Spinsters Ink

All The Muscle You Need, Diana McRae	$8.95
As You Desire, Madeline Moore	$9.95
Being Someone, Ann MacLeod	$9.95
Cancer in Two Voices, Butler & Rosenblum	$12.95
Child of Her People, Anne Cameron	$8.95
Considering Parenthood, Cheri Pies	$12.95
Desert Years, Cynthia Rich	$7.95
Elise, Claire Kensington	$7.95
Final Rest, Mary Morell	$9.95
Final Session, Mary Morell	$9.95
High and Outside, Linnea A. Due	$8.95
The Journey, Anne Cameron	$9.95
The Lesbian Erotic Dance, JoAnn Loulan	$12.95
Lesbian Passion, JoAnn Loulan	$12.95
Lesbian Sex, JoAnn Loulan	$12.95
Lesbians at Midlife, ed. by Sang, Warshow & Smith	$12.95
Life Savings, Linnea Due	$10.95
Look Me in the Eye, 2nd Ed., Macdonald & Rich	$8.95
Love and Memory, Amy Oleson	$9.95
Modern Daughters and the Outlaw West, Melissa Kwasny	$9.95
The Solitary Twist, Elizabeth Pincus	$9.95
Thirteen Steps, Bonita L. Swan	$8.95
The Two-Bit Tango, Elizabeth Pincus	$9.95
Vital Ties, Karen Kringle	$10.95
Why Can't Sharon Kowalski Come Home? Thompson & Andrzejewski	$10.95

Spinsters titles are available at your local booksellers, or by mail order through Spinsters Ink. A free catalogue is available upon request.

Please include $1.50 for the first title ordered, and 50 cents for every title thereafter. Visa and Mastercard accepted.

Spinsters Ink was founded in 1978 to produce vital books for diverse women's communities. In 1986 we merged with Aunt Lute Books to become Spinsters/Aunt Lute. In 1990, the Aunt Lute Foundation became an independent non-profit publishing program. In 1992, Spinsters moved to Minneapolis.

Spinsters Ink is committed to publishing full-length novels and non-fiction works that deal with significant issues in women's lives from a feminist perspective: books that not only name crucial issues in women's lives, but more importantly encourage change and growth; books that help make the best in our lives more possible. We are particularly interested in creative works by lesbians.

spinsters ink, p.o. box 300170, minneapolis, mn 55403